THE PLAYBOY'S RUTHLESS PURSUIT

BY
MIRANDA LEE

MILLS & BOON

First Published in Great Britain 2016
By Mills & Boon, an imprint of HarperCollins*Publishers*
1 London Bridge Street, London, SE1 9GF

© 2016 Miranda Lee

ISBN: 978-0-263-91633-1

Our policy is to use papers that are natural, renewable and recyclable
products and made from wood grown in sustainable forests. The logging
regulations of the country of origin.

Printed and bound in Spain
by CPI, Barcelona

Born and raised in the Australian bush, **Miranda Lee** was boarding-school-educated, and briefly pursued a career in classical music before moving to Sydney and embracing the world of computers. Happily married, with three daughters, she began writing when family commitments kept her at home. She likes to create stories that are believable, modern, fast-paced and sexy. Her interests include meaty sagas, doing word puzzles, gambling and going to the movies.

To my husband, Tony,
for always being there.

CHAPTER ONE

I SHOULD BE HAPPIER, Jeremy thought as he leant back in his office chair and put his feet up on his large leather-topped desk. *My life is pretty well perfect. I'm as healthy as a horse, filthy rich and blessedly single. On top of that, I'm no longer Chief Investment Consultant at the London branch of the Barker-Whittle banking empire. What a relief!*

Working for his over-achieving father had not been Jeremy's idea of a fun occupation. Unfortunately, he'd been darned good at his job. Despite the accolades and the generous bonuses he'd earned over the years, he much preferred being his own boss. Jeremy had used some of his recently acquired wealth to buy an ailing publishing firm, which he was turning into a rather surprising success. Perverse, considering it was an accidental purchase.

Jeremy's initial aim when launching out on his own had been to go into the property development business, his first purchase last year a town house in one of Mayfair's best streets. But the publishing company leasing the building had proved difficult to deal with, the owner stubbornly insisting on staying put till his lease ran out. So Jeremy had made an offer that he couldn't refuse, thereby solving the problem, his intention having been to relocate his new business to cheaper premises whilst he renovated and converted the slightly run-down property into three luxury apartments.

But things hadn't worked out that way. He'd found himself *liking* the people who worked at Mayfair Books, all of whom were naturally worried about losing their jobs. He also liked the rooms the way they were. Slightly shabby, yes, but full of character and charm, with lots of wood-panelled walls and antique furniture. It had been clear from talking to the employees and looking at their sales figures, however, that the business itself had desperately needed updating. Whilst Jeremy had known next to nothing about the modern publishing industry, he was an intelligent and well-connected man, with loads of business contacts, one of which headed the marketing division of a rather famous London publisher.

So here he was, almost a year later, heading Barker Books, having changed the name along with the company's fortunes. They'd actually made a profit during the last quarter. He even got up every morning and happily went into his office these days, unlike his time at the bank when he'd conducted most of his business over the phone.

So work wasn't the reason for this odd feeling of discontent.

Jeremy knew it wasn't his love life, either. That was sailing along as usual, though, since buying the book business, his focus had been more on work than women.

Not that he felt sexually frustrated. He didn't. Jeremy had no trouble finding willing ladies to accompany him to the many social occasions he was constantly invited to. A man of his status and wealth was a prized guest. His partner du jour invariably accompanied him back to his bed for the night, despite Jeremy always making it clear that dating him was never going to lead to a ring on her finger. He didn't do love or, God forbid, marriage. Thankfully, most of them were good with that, because he didn't do broken hearts, either.

When the reason for his discontent continued to elude Jeremy, he was forced to give the matter deeper thought, something he usually tried to avoid at all costs. He'd never seen the benefit of self-analysis, or counselling. It had never done his older brothers any good. Jeremy knew exactly why he was the way he was. He didn't need a shrink to tell him that his aversion to love and marriage stemmed from his parents' constant divorcing and remarrying. That, plus their abandoning him to boarding school when he was just eight, where he'd been bullied endlessly.

He hated thinking about those years, so he didn't, his mind swiftly moving on to happier times. He'd thoroughly enjoyed his years at University in London, finally using his excellent brain to its full capacity. His results had thrilled his maternal grandmother, who'd promptly made him her heir, on the condition he went on to study at Oxford. Which he had, his generous private income—Gran had passed away shortly after he enrolled—providing him with the kind of lifestyle to which he'd quickly become addicted. He'd done sufficient study to easily pass his exams but, generally speaking, fun had been the order of the day, Jeremy carousing to a level that might have become a problem if he hadn't acquired two slightly more sensible friends.

Thinking of Sergio and Alex sent Jeremy's gaze to the photo of the three of them that was sitting on his desk. Harriet had taken it on the day Sergio had married his one-time stepsister in July last year, Sergio having asked both Alex and himself to be his best men. The wedding had taken place on the shores of Lake Como, in the grounds of a magnificent villa. Whilst no longer worried that Bella might be a chip off her fortune-hunting mother's block, Jeremy wasn't convinced the marriage would last. Love never lasted, did it? Still, there was nothing he could do about that. It was a shame, though, how little he saw of his best friend these days. Of *both* his best friends. He *had* seen them at Alex's wedding to Harriet in Australia back in February, but only briefly. Jeremy really missed the days when they'd all lived in London and got together regularly, back when they'd still all been bachelors and hadn't become billionaires.

Hadn't been thirty-five, either. That had been the kiss of death, their all turning thirty-five last year. That, and the super sale of their WOW wine bar franchise to an American equity company. Suddenly, everything had changed, with the Bachelor Club they'd formed back at Oxford no longer relevant. Maybe their friendship was no longer relevant, either.

With a sigh, Jeremy scraped his feet off his desk. They hit the floor with a thud, the sound echoing the hollow feeling inside his heart. Leaning forward, he picked up the photo, frowning as he studied the three faces smiling back at him.

Jeremy didn't envy his friends and their marriages, but he hated the thought that he would hardly ever see them from now on. Their priorities would be their wives and their families, not him. He would become old news, someone whom they recalled with vague fondness when they glanced through their photo albums every decade or so.

'Who's that man, Dad?' he imagined Alex's son asking. Harriet was expecting a boy.

'Oh, that's Jeremy. A chap I knew once. We went to Oxford together. He was the best man at our wedding. Gosh. Haven't seen him for years.'

Jeremy scowled as he slammed the photo face down on the desk and snatched up his phone.

'Damn it all, I'm not going to let that happen,' he ground out as he retrieved Alex's number.

Realising it would be the middle of the night in Australia—not nice to call at such an hour—Jeremy sent an email volunteering himself for godfather duty when the time came. That done, he righted the photo, placed it back in its pride of place and settled down to have a look at their current sales figures. Finding the file on his laptop, he clicked it open but didn't get far before there was a rapid *tap-tap-tap* on his door.

'Come in, Madge,' he said.

Madge entered as briskly as she did everything. In her mid-fifties, Madge was a thin, plain woman with cropped grey hair, piercing blue eyes and a schoolmarm manner.

Jeremy had hired her soon after buying the business, the previous owner's secretary having quit in a huff over the new owner's high-handed tactics. Jeremy had been impressed with Madge's no-nonsense attitude, plus her knowledge of the publishing industry. He liked her enormously, and the affection was mutual.

'We have a problem,' she said straight away.

'Which is?'

'Kenneth Jacobs can't be the auctioneer at tonight's charity auction. He has a terrible head cold. I could hardly understand him on the phone just now.'

'I see,' Jeremy said, not actually seeing at all. He knew who Kenneth Jacobs was; hard not to, since he was Jeremy's only best-selling author, having come with the deal when he'd bought the business. Kenneth wrote the grizzliest of murder mysteries, which had a huge fan base but whose forty-plus books hadn't been marketed properly. Despite knowing this, Kenneth hadn't left the publisher who'd given him his start. A crusty old bachelor, Kenneth was lazy when it came to business matters. Once Jeremy had taken the helm, he'd republished Kenneth's entire back list, with new covers, and put them all out as e-Books.

'What charity auction?' Jeremy asked, having gained the impression that he was supposed to already know.

Madge rolled her eyes. 'Truly. Just as well you have me to organise things around here. It's not easy working for a man who has a short-term memory loss.'

'I'll have you know I have a photographic memory,' Jeremy said defensively whilst his mind scrambled to remember what it was he'd forgotten.

'In that case I'll photograph everything for you in the future instead of telling you,' Madge said with her usual caustic wit.

As much as Jeremy often enjoyed Madge's dry sense of humour, on this occasion his patience was wearing a little thin.

'Do that, Madge. But for now I would appreciate it if you'd explain about this charity auction one more time, then tell me exactly how I'm supposed to fix the problem of Kenneth having a head cold.' Though by now he had a pretty good idea. Jeremy wasn't always the most intuitive of men, but he wasn't thick, either.

Madge expelled one of her exasperated sighs. 'I would have thought that the words *charity auction* were self-explanatory. But that's beside the point. You told me after the last charity dinner you went to that I wasn't to accept any more invitations to such dos. You said you'd rather slash your wrists than sit through another of those dinners where the food was below par and the speakers intolerably boring. You said you were happy to donate to whatever cause was going but you'd given up being a masochist when you stopped working for your father. You said that—'

'Yes, yes,' Jeremy broke in firmly. 'I get the picture. But that last dinner was just a meal followed by speeches, not something as interesting as an auction. Now, if you don't mind, please fill me in on the relevant details and stop with the ancient history lesson.'

Madge looked as close to sheepish as he'd ever seen her. 'Right. Well, it's being held in the ballroom of the Chelsea Hotel, and it's to raise funds for the women's refuges in the inner-city area. There's a sit-down dinner before the auction, which I'm assured will have quality food and which should raise a good sum of money since it costs a small fortune per head. I gather the place is going to be full of society's finest. Kenneth was to be the auctioneer, the last prize being the privilege of the winning bidder having their name used as a character in his next book. It's been done before, of course, by other authors. But never by Kenneth. The poor fellow is quite disappointed, as well as worried about letting Alice down. She's the girl who's organised everything. Anyway, I told him that you would do it in his stead.'

Jeremy pretended to look displeased. 'Oh, you did, did you?'

For a split second, a worried frown formed on Madge's high forehead. But then she smiled.

'You're just joking, right?'

Jeremy grinned.

Madge flushed with relief and pleasure. She adored Jeremy, envying his mother for having such a warm and wonderful son. He might be a devil where the ladies were concerned—or so she'd been told—but he was a good man and a great boss. Smart, sensible and surprisingly sensitive. She didn't doubt that one day he'd fall in love and settle down.

'You are a teaser,' she said. 'Now, do you want me to ring Alice and tell her you'll do the job as auctioneer? Or do you want to ring her yourself?'

'What do you think, Madge?'

This was another thing she liked about her boss. He often asked her opinion. And usually took it.

'I think you should ring her yourself,' she said. 'It would put her mind at rest. She seemed rather stressed. I gained the impression she was new at this job.'

'Right,' he replied, nodding. 'You'd better get me her number, then.'

Madge already had it in hand, of course.

'You are a very devious woman,' he said as she gave it to him.

'And you are a very sweet man,' she returned with a smug smile before turning and leaving him to it.

Jeremy found himself smiling as he keyed Alice's number into his phone.

'Alice Waterhouse,' she answered immediately, her voice crisp and very businesslike, its cut-glass accent betraying an education at one of those private girls' schools that turned out girls who invariably worked in jobs such as PR or fund-raising for charities before marrying someone suitable to their class.

Jeremy wasn't overly keen on girls from privileged backgrounds, which was rather hypocritical of him, given his own background. There'd been a time when he hadn't cared about such things. If a girl was pretty and keen on him, then he didn't give their character—or their upbringing—much thought. He bedded without bias or prejudice. But nowadays, he found the girls he dated who'd been born rich were seriously boring, both in bed and out. He disliked their innate sense of entitlement, plus their need to be constantly complimented and entertained. Perhaps it was the attraction of opposites, but there was something very appealing about girls who *had* to work for their living, who didn't have the fall-back position of Daddy's money.

He imagined that the plummy-voiced Alice Waterhouse was just such a daddy's girl.

'Jeremy Barker-Whittle,' he replied, well aware that whilst his own voice wasn't overly toffee-nosed, it was deep and rich and, yes, impressive. Alex and Sergio used to tell him he could have made a fortune on the radio. People who first met him over the phone were often surprised by the reality of him in the flesh. They clearly expected someone older, and possibly more rotund, with a big chest and stomach. Like an opera singer.

People did make the wrong assumptions at times.

He wondered if he was wrong about Alice Waterhouse. Then decided he wasn't.

'I'm the publisher of Kenneth Jacobs's books,' he informed her. 'It seems I'm to be your stand-in auctioneer tonight.'

'Oh, that's wonderful,' she said, not gushing but obviously relieved. 'Madge said you might do it. I have to confess I was beginning to panic. Thank you so much.'

Against his better judgment, Jeremy found himself warming to her.

'It's my pleasure,' he said. 'Truly.' Jeremy had always fancied himself a bit of a showman. He would actually enjoy playing auctioneer tonight.

'You can bring a partner, if you wish,' Alice offered. 'I allocated two places for Mr Jacobs at the main dining table. He said he didn't have anyone to bring so I was going to sit with him.'

'I won't be bringing anyone with me, either,' Jeremy admitted. He might have brought Ellen, a lawyer he dated on and off, and whose company he enjoyed. But she was overseas in Washington, working, at the moment. 'I'm a crusty old bachelor too,' he added, amused by this description of himself. 'So perhaps you would do me the honour of sitting next to me at dinner tonight.'

'That would be *my* pleasure,' she returned.

'I presume it's black tie?'

'Yes, it is. Is that a problem?'

Jeremy smiled wryly. 'No. No problem.' If there was one thing for which Jeremy could be relied upon it was to show up at social functions, properly attired. He loved fashion, and took pride in his appearance. His wardrobe held a wide array of clothes from casual to formal. His dinner suits were the best money could buy, the one he'd worn to Sergio's wedding made by one of the top tailors in Milan. He'd wear that one tonight.

When she started thanking him again, he cut her short by asking when and where they could meet up tonight. Once he had the details in hand, he said goodbye, hung up then called out to Madge.

She popped her head through the door straight away.

'Everything settled?' she asked.

'Fine. Just tell me one thing. Have you actually met this Alice?'

'No. I only talked to her over the phone.'

'So what PR company does she work for?'

Madge looked puzzled. 'She doesn't. I mean...didn't

I tell you? She works as a counsellor at a couple of the women's refuges.'

'No, Madge, you didn't mention that.'

'Sorry. Bit flustered today. Anyway, Alice explained when she first rang that they couldn't afford the fees of professional fund-raisers so she was doing it all herself. Not an easy job, I can assure you.'

'No,' Jeremy said thoughtfully. Damn, but he hated it when he was wrong about someone. He supposed it wasn't impossible that the daughters of wealthy men could be born with social consciences, plus the desire to make a difference to those less fortunate than themselves. But in his experience, it was rare.

Jeremy was impressed, and resolved to do everything in his power to make tonight's auction a success.

'I'd better get back to work,' he said, but his mind remained elsewhere. He was definitely looking forward to finding out tonight all about the enigmatic and intriguing Alice Waterhouse.

CHAPTER TWO

'THANK YOU FOR lending me this lovely cocktail dress, Fiona,' Alice said as she inspected herself in the cheval mirror. The dress was black and sleek and strapless, with a matching coat that would protect her from the chill night air till she could get inside the air-conditioned hotel. Despite summer being just over a month away, London was in the grip of a cold snap.

'My pleasure,' her flatmate replied, the words reminding Alice of the conversation she'd had earlier today with Kenneth Jacobs's publisher. What a nice man he was. And what a lovely voice. He would make a much better auctioneer than Mr Jacobs.

'I seriously wish I was going to your do tonight instead of having dinner with Alistair's parents,' Fiona added. 'But it's his mother's birthday...' Her voice trailed off as she shrugged resignedly. 'Never a good idea to get on the wrong foot with one's future mother-in-law.'

'I would imagine not,' Alice agreed, glad that she'd never have to worry about such matters. No way was she ever going to get married.

'You look lovely,' Fiona said. 'I wish I had your figure. And your height. And your hair.'

Alice was taken aback by the compliments, thinking there wasn't anything special about her figure, though she did have nice hair, naturally blonde and easy to style. As for her height, she wasn't that tall. Just under five eight. Admittedly, Fiona was on the short side. Despite that, she was a strikingly attractive girl with thick dark hair, big brown eyes and the kind of voluptuous body that men lusted after. Not that Alice wanted to be lusted after. It was the last thing she wanted.

'That dress looks much better on you than it did on me,' Fiona went on. 'When I wore it, my boobs spilled out over the top. I had men gawking at them all night. Alistair said I was never to wear it again, so if you want it, sweetie, it's yours.'

Alice hated the way Fiona called her sweetie, as if she were a kid when in fact they were both the same age. She also didn't want to be treated as if she were still the girl who'd first come to London and shown up, broke, on the doorstep. Still, it was an understandable hangover from when Alice had first come to London and shown up, broke, on the doorstep of Fiona's flat, mainly because she was the closest thing to a friend that Alice had ever had at boarding school. Not that they moved in the same circles, but they did share crushes on the same movie stars. Alice had only known Fiona's address because Fiona had told everyone at school when her billionaire father had presented her with the keys of a Kensington flat for her eighteenth birthday.

To give Fiona credit, she'd taken Alice in and let her have a room, rent-free, till Alice had been able to earn some money. Then, when Alice had said she would be moving out a few weeks later, Fiona had begged her to stay, saying she enjoyed her company. Over the seven years they'd lived together, they'd become quite close, sharing confidences the way girls did. Fiona understood why Alice was anti-men, but she still hadn't given up hope that one day Alice would meet a man she could trust—and love.

'Did I tell you that Kenneth Jacobs pulled out of doing the auctioneer job at the last minute?' Alice said as Fiona sprayed her with perfume. 'He came down with a head cold.'

'Oh, no!' Fiona exclaimed. 'What did you do?'

'I panicked at first.'

Fiona laughed. 'You? Panic? Never! You would have sorted something out.'

Fiona's blind faith in her organisational skills amused Alice. Still, anyone would seem cool, calm and collected in comparison with Fiona, who could be quite scatter-brained. And very messy. It crossed Alice's mind that Fiona might have originally asked her to stay because she did most of the housework.

'I was lucky. Kenneth put me onto this lovely lady at Barker Books and before I knew it, the owner of the company rang me back and offered to take Mr Jacobs's place.'

'That *was* lucky.'

'You've no idea how lucky. He has this absolutely gorgeous voice. He's going to make a great auctioneer. Now no more of that perfume, Fiona. I have to get my things together. The cab I ordered will be here any second. I've made arrangements to meet Mr Barker-Whittle in the foyer of the hotel at seven.'

'What?'

'I said I—'

'I know what you said,' Fiona broke in sharply. 'I hope we're not talking about *Jeremy* Barker-Whittle here.'

Alice frowned. 'Yes. That's how he introduced himself. Why? What's the matter with him?'

'He's just one of the most infamous playboys in London—that's what's the matter with him. Handsome as the devil, with more charm than any man has a right to. My sister dated him once for about five minutes, and she hasn't stopped raving about him ever since. She claims that after being with Jeremy no other man could possibly compare. Lord, but I'd never have lent you that sexy dress if I knew who you'd be sitting next to tonight.'

Whilst momentarily thrown by this news, Alice also felt peeved that Fiona would think for a moment she would fall victim to some playboy's dubious charms. Surely she knew her better than that. Now that she'd been warned about Mr

Barker-Whittle, he had not a hope in Hades of snaring her interest, no matter how handsome and charming he was. And he *was* charming, she conceded, thinking of how much she'd liked him over the phone. And yes, he was a right royal devil, calling himself a crusty old bachelor like that!

'Forewarned is forearmed, Fiona,' she pointed out. 'Now that I know he's a player, I will be on guard against any attempt by him to seduce me. Though you, of all people, should know I am immune to men of his type.'

Even as she said the words, Alice knew she was lying. She'd always found handsome devils attractive. In the movies mostly, but also in real life. There was something wickedly appealing about good-looking men of a certain reputation. She'd gone out with one once, and it had cost her dearly. Whilst still not totally immune to finding such men attractive, she felt confident she had learned her lesson. It was a pity, however, that her stand-in auctioneer was coming alone. Still, if Jeremy Barker-Whittle decided after meeting her that she would provide him with some after-auction entertainment, then he was sadly mistaken.

'But I don't get it,' Fiona said. 'Jeremy's in banking, not books.'

'Well, he's in books now,' Alice said ruefully whilst wishing that he weren't. What a pity Kenneth had to come down with a cold.

'Strange,' Fiona mused. 'Still, I suppose he can afford to be in anything he wants to be in. The Barker-Whittle family is seriously loaded. They've been in merchant banking forever.'

'You seem to know a lot about them.'

'Yes, well, as I said, Melody became obsessed with the man for a while and made it her business to find out everything she could.'

'Anything else I should know about him before tonight?' Alice asked.

'Not really. Just don't believe a word the silver-tongued scoundrel says. And don't go agreeing to go out with him.'

Alice almost laughed. As if.

'That'll be my cab,' she said when her phone pinged. 'Now you have a nice time tonight, Fiona, and don't worry about me. I'll be fine. Jeremy Barker-Whittle won't even get to first base.'

Fiona didn't look so sure. Alice recalled her friend's worried expression when she walked into the foyer of the hotel a couple of minutes past seven. *Fiona had a right to be worried*, came the instant stomach-tightening thought.

Jeremy Barker-Whittle was already there, sitting on one of the guest sofas, talking to someone on his phone. She knew it was him, despite the presence of several other males in the foyer. None of them, however, was wearing a black dinner suit. And none fitted the image she'd already formed in her mind of what one of London's most infamous playboys would look like. When Fiona had been talking about him, Alice had automatically pictured one of her favourite movie stars who'd made his reputation by playing rich bad boys. Jeremy Barker-Whittle was almost a dead ringer. Very handsome with an elegance to his face and clothes that could not be feigned. He had money written all over him, the kind of man whom other men envied and women craved.

Alice didn't crave him, but his looks certainly set her heart racing. She scooped in a deep breath, glad that he hadn't noticed her yet. It gave her the opportunity to gather her wits and her defences. And to look him over without being observed. His mid-brown hair was slightly wavy; it fell from a side part to his collar, a single lock flopping sexily across his high forehead. His nose was strong and straight and his eyes a sparkling blue. Yes, they actually sparkled. At least they did when he glanced up and spied her standing there, looking at him. He immediately put his phone away and stood up, smiling as he came over to her, bringing her attention to his mouth, with its sensual lower lip and dazzlingly white teeth. Now her stomach did a little flip-flop, reminding her starkly of her vulnerability to men who looked perfect but invariably were not.

'Please tell me that you're Alice,' he said with that incredible voice of his. Like rich dark chocolate, it actually made her name sound sexy. Which was a minor miracle. She'd always hated her name, thinking it girlish and old-fashioned.

It was difficult not to respond to his practised charm, but she managed to control herself, tapping into the reserved façade that she always used around men of his ilk.

'I am,' she admitted coolly, having resisted the unwise impulse to smile back at him. 'And I presume you're Mr Barker-Whittle?'

CHAPTER THREE

WHOA! THOUGHT JEREMY. He wasn't used to women being this cool to him, especially women who looked like Alice. It rattled him for a moment. But only a moment, his mind searching for some reason why she might be in a negative frame of mind where he was concerned. All he could think of was the way he'd described himself as a crusty old bachelor. Maybe she didn't like being deceived. She'd been warm enough to him over the phone, whereas now she was all ice.

The corner of his mouth twisted at his own pun on her name. Alice. All ice. *Very funny, Jeremy. Now see if you can use some of the infamous Barker-Whittle charm to warm up Miss Ice Princess a bit, or the evening ahead is not going to be as enjoyable as you anticipated.*

Which was a shame, given that he was partial to slender, cool-looking blondes, especially ones with gorgeous blue eyes and mouths just made for sin.

'Please, call me Jeremy,' he insisted as he subtly looked her up and down. 'No one calls me Mr Barker-Whittle, not even Madge. Especially not Madge,' he added with a laugh. 'By the way, Madge said that we should offer two character names to auction off, not just one,' he invented. 'If that's all right with you.'

'What? Oh, yes. Yes. That would be…great. Thank you.'

He'd thrown her a little, which was exactly what he'd wanted to do. For a split second she was the Alice he'd talked to on the phone. Sweet and grateful. But then that chilly mask slipped back into place.

Not that Jeremy was giving up. He had all evening to accomplish the thawing of Alice. If nothing else, he would enjoy the challenge. After all, it wasn't every day that a member of the opposite sex challenged him, especially single ones. He'd duly noted the lack of rings on either hand, a sure sign that she was neither married nor engaged. Of course, that didn't mean she didn't have a boyfriend or a partner. Though surely any boyfriend or partner worth his salt would have accompanied her here tonight. If one existed and he'd made a deliberate choice not to come, then the fool deserved to lose out. On second thought, however, Jeremy doubted there was some man waiting in the wings. That air of touch-me-not that she had about her would not encourage the average modern male.

Jeremy smiled wryly at the knowledge that he was far from average, or in the slightest deterred in his pursuit of the gorgeous Alice. She'd sparked curiosity in him from the first moment he'd heard that cut-glass voice of hers. Now that he'd met her, his curiosity was joined by desire, Jeremy resolving not to rest till she agreed to go out with him.

'You were going to show me the layout in the ballroom,' he reminded her. 'But first, let me take your coat...'

Panic churned in Alice's stomach at the thought of taking her coat off, of exposing more of herself to this man's far too sexy gaze. If he thought she hadn't noticed the way he'd looked her over, he was sadly mistaken. Alice knew men found her attractive. It was a burden most blondes with nice figures and pretty faces had to put up with. Fortunately, these days, she didn't attract too much male attention, always going to work with her hair pulled back, no make-up on and wearing jeans. Tonight, however, she was looking her very best. Silently, she cursed Fiona for lending her this revealing dress, plus spraying her with all that expensive perfume. The make-up she only had herself to blame for. But at the time, she hadn't known she'd be spending the evening in the company of a man who could make her want to be different from the woman she'd become.

At least she'd put her hair up, though not into its usual scraped-back ponytail. It was fashioned into a sleek sophisticated bun, worn slightly on one side, the latest style for formal occasions. Still, better than it being down. Pity about the dangling diamanté earrings she'd chosen to wear, however, and which swung against her bare neck when she walked. Alice contemplated telling him she would keep her coat on but he was already moving behind her and, really, she could hardly go all night with a calf-length coat flapping around her legs. Without glancing over her shoulder at him, she reached up to push the coat back off her shoulders—it wasn't the kind that had buttons—sucking in sharply when she felt his fingertips brush over the nape of her neck. A shiver ricocheted down her spine as the coat slid down her arms, presumably into his waiting hands. She was too shaken to turn and look. Too shocked.

What kind of power did this man have to make her feel like this? So swiftly and so surely. Alice had felt sexual attraction before; she hadn't always been so wary of it. She'd found the thought of sex fascinating from the time puberty hit, spending a lot of her teenage years indulging in romantic fantasies over various handsome actors. Then there'd been that charmer at college, the tall dark and handsome one she'd been attracted to despite everything, the one who'd convinced her he returned her feelings. And so she'd agreed to go out with him. More fool her!

But the attraction she'd felt on that occasion paled into insignificance compared to this highly charged feeling that was currently sweeping through Alice. It was madness, this urge she had to throw caution to the winds, to forget all the lessons she'd learned about men, to ignore Fiona's warnings and just let Jeremy Barker-Whittle have his wicked way with her. Which, of course, was what he wanted to do. He was a playboy, wasn't he? That was what playboys did.

But not with me, Alice decided as she marshalled all her willpower. *Not tonight. Not* ever.

'I'll just go over and check this in,' he said smoothly after she turned to finally look at him. 'Then we can proceed.'

He walked the same way he did everything, she noted ruefully. With style and casual elegance. Nothing hurried. Nothing awkward. Far too soon he was walking back towards her, this time his gaze openly admiring.

'Nothing beats a little black dress, does it?' he said as he took her elbow and steered her over to the bank of lifts. 'The concierge informed me that the ballroom is on the first floor,' he added, before she could ask what in hell he was doing. Not that she would have phrased it like that.

Still, she extricated her arm from his hold as soon as possible, sending him a look that held the silent but definite message that he was to keep his hands to himself. No way was she going to let him take control of the evening. Or of her. No way!

Jeremy resisted the temptation to roll his eyes. But truly, she was like a heroine out of a Victorian romance novel. Not that he'd read any, but he could imagine what such a woman would be like. All prissy and uptight, looking down her nose at men, especially ones who dared put a finger on her virginal flesh.

Alice would have been perfect for such a role, except for three factors. First, that dress. Strapless and very fitted, it gave him a clear picture of what she would look like naked. Very nice indeed, with high firm breasts, an athletically flat stomach, a deliciously small waist, long shapely legs and just enough hip and bottom for stroking. Second was the way she'd stared at him when she'd first arrived. That was not the stare of some prissy virgin. Her eyes had fairly ogled him, betraying that she'd found him as sexually attractive as he found her.

And then there was the way her whole body had quivered when his hand had brushed the back of her neck. It had been quite accidental. Jeremy wasn't in the habit of indulging in sly, lecherous touching. He never needed to. That Alice had reacted in such a way had been very telling. The woman who'd wrenched out of his hold just now should have whirled around and glared her disapproval. But she hadn't.

During the short ride up to the first floor in the lift, Jeremy concluded that Alice Waterhouse was nothing but a fraud. Her Ice Princess act with him was just that. An act. What was behind this pretence, he had no idea. But he aimed to find out.

CHAPTER FOUR

THE BALLROOM WAS INDEED, Alice already knew, on the first floor. She'd been there earlier today, checking that everything was being set up according to her instructions. She'd also taken personal responsibility for putting the name cards in place, having paid great attention to the guests' wishes when it came to seating. Each card also doubled as an auction number, being T-shaped, with the guest's name on the front and their number on the back.

Alice exited the lift first, anxious not to give Jeremy the opening to take her arm once more. She hated having to be rude, but she would be, if she had to. And she would *have* to if he kept manhandling her, his touch doing things to her body that didn't bear thinking about.

'It's just along here,' she said, and hurried down the carpeted corridor.

He kept up with her easily, his stride almost twice one of hers. Of course, he was a good six inches taller than she was, with long legs. Plus she couldn't walk all that fast in four-inch heels and a short, tight skirt.

The corridor eventually opened out into a larger space where a couple of staff members were putting the finishing touches to a bar area along one wall.

'Pre-dinner drinks are scheduled from seven-thirty onwards,' Alice said crisply as she walked over and pulled open one of the closed double doors that led into the ballroom, her eyes finally forced to meet those of her companion. 'The official time for the dinner to start is eight-thirty. I asked you to be here at seven so that you would have time to read through the list of items to be auctioned, and to discuss how you might want to proceed.'

'Proceed?' he echoed in that wonderfully rich voice of his, stepping forward to hold the door open for her.

Alice smothered a sigh. Trust him to have gallant manners. She supposed it was part of his seductive armoury to play the gentleman with women. No doubt he would pull out chairs and hold taxi doors open. And *always* wear a condom.

Alice only just managed not to gasp at this last thought. Where in heaven's name had that come from? Okay, so she found Jeremy Barker-Whittle attractive. Any woman would. He was drop-dead gorgeous. But finding him attractive was a far cry from thinking about having sex with him. Yet, as her gaze dropped from his beautiful blue eyes to his wickedly sexy mouth, she couldn't help wonder what it would be like to go to bed with him. He must be good at it, she reasoned, if Fiona's sister hadn't stopped raving about him. She'd met Fiona's sister, who was a real party girl. She'd sleep with anything in trousers, according to Fiona. So Melody must have slept with Jeremy.

'Cat got your tongue?' he said with a wry smile.

Alice blinked, swallowed, then shot him a small, stiff smile. 'Sorry. I had this sudden awful thought which distracted me.'

'Anything I should know about?'

'Not at all,' she said, thankful that she wasn't a blusher these days. She had been once, but not any longer. Working in women's refuges had toughened her up considerably. 'I've been a little OCD about the seating arrangements for dinner and it suddenly occurred to me that I might have made a mistake on one table.' Lord, but she was better at lying than she would ever have imagined. 'Still, nothing that can't be rectified,' she went on. 'Now, what I meant by how to proceed is do you want to have the whole auction after dinner, or sell off a few items between courses?'

'Definitely sell off a few items between courses. It will

keep the guests in a buying mood. And stop them from getting bored.'

'I agree. Right. Follow me.'

Jeremy followed her into the ballroom, appreciating the sight of her satin-encased derrière much more than her still less than warm demeanour. The ice in her voice and eyes might have melted a little but there was still a long way to go before he could confidently engage her in a conversation that might satisfy his curiosity over her, as well as give him an opening to ask her out. Still, he had several hours in which to achieve his goal.

Alice led him between a myriad of circular tables, each one set to a high standard with white linen tablecloths, silver cutlery, crystal glasses and beautifully appointed name cards placed at each setting. Every table had a number in the centre, which no doubt had been emailed to the guests so that they knew where to head on entering. That was what had happened at the last charity dinner Jeremy had been to, the one that had bored him to tears.

He already knew that this evening's dinner would not bore him in the slightest. In fact, Jeremy was looking forward to every intriguing second.

'It all looks splendid,' he complimented in Alice's wake.

She didn't stop or turn around, just said a cool, 'Yes, it does…' over her shoulder.

Jeremy frowned, wondering exactly what was bugging the lovely Miss Waterhouse. Surely she didn't act like this with every man she met. Was it him personally, or something else? Maybe she'd had a row with someone. The missing boyfriend perhaps?

'You organised all this by yourself?' he threw after her.

'Most of it,' she tossed back at him. 'The hotel staff were very helpful, of course.'

They arrived at the stage, which ran across the far end of the ballroom and which could be used for many purposes. Concerts. Award nights. Presentations. Whatever. Tonight it was set up with a podium in the middle, a microphone attached. There was a long wooden table behind it, which held an array of objects and a laptop computer, open, at one end. Clearly, this was where Alice would be standing, handing him items and jotting down the numbers of the winning bidder.

A man wouldn't want to be of a nervous disposition, Jeremy thought as he glanced up at the podium. Fortunately, he wasn't. But he wondered how Jacobs would have coped. Not that he knew the man well. Kenneth could be a secret exhibitionist for all he knew. Lazy did not mean shy.

There were three flights of steps, which led up onto the stage. One at each end and one in the middle. Alice stopped at the base of the one in the middle and finally turned to face him. She looked a little flushed in the face, but her eyes remained cool.

'I left the list of items for sale on the podium,' she told him. 'Perhaps you could have a look at them whilst I go check that seating.'

'Okay,' he agreed, and watched as she wound her way back through the tables, not stopping till she reached the one nearest the door, at which point he shrugged and made his way up onto the stage.

The list of items was extensive and varied. Sporting and entertainment memorabilia. Several dinners for two at five-star restaurants. A family weekend at a B&B in Weymouth. A short holiday for two in Spain. Premiere seats to a rock concert. Return flights to various European capitals. An oil painting of the Duchess of Cambridge by an up-and-coming London artist. Last but not least was the privilege of having Kenneth use a person's name—amend that to two—in his next thriller.

Jeremy didn't take long to scan the list, replacing it on the podium before taking a moment to inspect the wooden gavel, even giving it a practice bang, which echoed through the cavernous room and had several waiters lifting their heads for a moment. Not Alice, however, who was already no longer at the table near the doors. Jeremy wondered if that had just been an excuse not to remain in his company longer than strictly necessary. His teeth clenched in his jaw as he made his way down from the stage and headed for the exit. Frankly, he was beginning to feel slightly peeved. And confused. What was it about him that she didn't like? He wasn't used to women not liking him. He certainly wasn't used to being given the cold shoulder.

Jeremy soon saw that Alice wasn't outside in the pre-dinner drinks area, either. People had begun to arrive, but it wasn't crowded enough for him not to spot her. Creamy blonde hair like hers did stand out.

'Jeremy Barker-Whittle!' a male voice boomed out from just behind his shoulder. 'Fancy seeing you here.'

Jeremy turned with some reluctance to face the owner of that voice. George Peterson had been a client of his when he'd been an investment consultant. The owner of several car yards, he had entrusted Jeremy with building his con-siderable savings into an early retirement portfolio. Fortu-nately, Jeremy had obliged. George was in his late fifties, his wife around the same age, Jeremy liking the fact that George hadn't traded his wife in for a younger model as most self-made men seemed to do at some stage.

George beamed at him. 'I was talking to Mandy here about you the other day, wasn't I, love? I said whatever am I going to do now that Jeremy's no longer looking after my money? I got so nervous last month that I cashed in all my stocks and shares and put them in the bank.'

'Not such a bad move, George. Things are very vola-tile at the moment. Still, your money's not going to grow much sitting in the bank. Perhaps you should think about buying property.'

'See, what did I tell you, love? Jeremy's always got his finger on the pulse. So what are you up to these days, lad? Got a proper girlfriend yet or are you still playing the field?'

It was ironic that Alice came into view right at that moment, smiling and chatting with people as she worked the room, a glass of champagne in her right hand. Their eyes met and Jeremy smiled at her, at which point George's ruddy face swivelled round to see what he was smiling at.

'*Very* nice,' George said, thankfully in a low voice. 'Is she your date for tonight?'

'No,' Jeremy admitted. 'She's the lady who's organised this do. Her name's Alice Waterhouse. Alice!' he called out, and beckoned her over. 'Come and meet some very good friends of mine,' he added, smiling at the thought that she could hardly avoid him now.

'I know Alice,' Mandy piped up. 'I spoke to her on the phone when I first got her email about tonight. When I told her how much a fan I was of Kenneth Jacobs's books, she said she'd put me on the same table as him.'

Alice plastered a smile on her face and went to meet Jeremy's very good friends.

Jeremy introduced them, Alice quickly remembering her phone conversation with Mandy.

'I'm so sorry,' she said straight away, glad to be able to direct her conversation towards anyone but the very annoying Jeremy, who continued to smile at her in that smug fashion, as though they had some kind of secret relationship going on. 'Mr Jacobs can't be here tonight. He's got a dreadful cold. We're still auctioning off his prize, though. His publisher here has very kindly agreed to do the auctioneering honours tonight.' With that, she served Jeremy with a saccharine smile that didn't touch her eyes.

'*What?*' George's eyes widened with surprise. 'Is she talking about you, Jeremy?'

'She is indeed.'

'When did you become a publisher?'

'Shortly after I left banking.'

'Is there money in it?'

'Probably not,' Jeremy said drily. 'But as they say in the classics, it's not always about the money.'

George guffawed. 'That's a good one. A Barker-Whittle saying it's not about the money.'

Alice noticed that Jeremy's eyes stopped sparkling for a split second. Not that she cared.

A waiter with a tray of drinks paused next to their group, offering them flutes of champagne or orange juice. They all selected champagne, all except Alice who already had a glass, which she was not actually drinking. She couldn't afford to get tipsy, not if she had to deal with lover boy all night. Her vain attempt to avoid him till dinner hadn't worked, she conceded with a degree of frustration.

'I really should mingle,' Alice said. 'I'll see you all at dinner, since we're on the same table.'

'How lovely!' Mandy gushed.

'I'll mingle with you,' Jeremy offered immediately.

'No need to do that,' Alice blurted out in alarm. 'You should stay and look after your friends.'

'We don't need looking after, little lady,' George retorted. 'Off you go, both of you.'

The conspiratorial smirk he sent Jeremy did not escape Alice's notice. Lord knew what he'd said to the man.

'Why did George look at you like that?' she asked bluntly as she made her way through the milling crowd, Jeremy at her side.

'Like what?'

She ground to a halt and glared up at him. 'Like he was secretly playing matchmaker.'

'Can't say that I noticed.'

Alice sighed in exasperation.

'George is a bit of a romantic,' he added. 'Take no notice of him.'

She was struggling to find something to say when Jeremy was claimed by another couple who knew him, this time some television executive and his wife. And that was how it went for the next forty minutes, lots of other guests vying for his attention as if he were some kind of celebrity, all of them assuming she was his girlfriend, something he occasionally didn't deny. Not that that stopped the women from flirting with him. Neither did it stop her feeling ridiculously, irrationally jealous.

Irritated and confused, Alice had difficulty maintaining her usual calm demeanour. Finally, the urge to snap something rather rude at an over-made-up blonde whose false eyelashes were in danger of falling off she was fluttering them so much, almost overwhelmed Alice. Sucking in a deep, gathering breath, she turned to Jeremy, smiling up at him in a somewhat brittle fashion. 'Sorry, Jeremy, but I must visit the ladies' room before the evening begins. I'll see you later at the table. Ours is table number one.'

The relief she felt at exiting his presence was enormous. But the sight of her over-bright eyes in the powder-room mirror was both telling and worrying. *Be careful, Alice*, she warned herself. *Be very, very careful.*

CHAPTER FIVE

JEREMY FOUND GEORGE and his wife before entering the ballroom at twenty-five minutes past eight, chatting away with them as they made their way to table one, which was right at the front of the room near the stage. Alice was nowhere to be seen, her continued absence frustrating him. Never one to beat a dead horse, Jeremy began to accept that perhaps Alice actually *wasn't* attracted to him. But if that was the case, why had she reacted negatively a couple of times to women flirting with him? And she had. Oh, yes. He'd glimpsed definite irritation in her body language, especially when that blonde had started giving him gooey-eyed looks.

Jeremy was thinking about the reasons for Alice cutting and running when she suddenly walked out onto the stage, making her way slowly towards the podium. How magnificent she looked up there, he thought, unable to take his eyes off her. Like a young Audrey Hepburn, though with blonde hair. Talk about class! Once in position at the podium she turned on the microphone and tapped it a couple of times, bringing relative quiet to the buzzing ballroom. Once everyone was seated, she cast a wide smile around the room and began to speak in that well-educated, crystal-clear voice of hers.

'Welcome, everyone,' she began. 'First, I must thank you all for coming here tonight and supporting a cause that is dear to my heart. It is unfortunate that women's refuges are necessary in our supposedly civilised and enlightened world, but that is sadly the case. Some of you might not know this, but I work as a counsellor at a few of the inner-city refuges, and I know personally that they are all struggling to make ends meet, plus to cope with the number of women asking for help. We desperately need more refuges. More case workers. More counsellors. Of course, that all means more money, some of which we hope to raise tonight through your kindness and generosity. So please...dig deep. Trust me when I say that whatever you donate will make a huge difference to those women who have nowhere to go and no one to turn to. They need your help. Thank you.'

When Alice stopped speaking, the whole room erupted with clapping, Jeremy feeling immensely proud of her, and quite moved. What a speech! What a woman! Politicians could take a leaf out of her book when it came to inspiring people. If he hadn't been doing the auctioneering job, Jeremy would have been tempted to bid for every single item himself, making sure that the very best price would be achieved before the gavel came down. As it was, he vowed to give the charity a hefty donation of his own at the end of the night. Who knew? Maybe the gesture would make her agree to go out with him. Because he was still going to ask her, wasn't he? Nothing was surer in his mind.

When Alice sat down at the table, everyone spoke to her at once, congratulating her on her lovely words and assuring her that they would all dig deep. Jeremy couldn't get a word in edgewise. As soon as he could, he leant a little closer to her and said quietly, 'That was a seriously impressive speech, Alice. You could do fund-raising for a career, if you wanted to.'

Alice stiffened at the way her body responded to that deeply masculine voice of his, plus the warmth of his breath against her ear. Her stomach tightened, and so did her nipples, something which had never happened to her before. It was quite frightening, but also insidiously beguiling. She ached to turn to him and give him a real smile, one which told him how desperately she wanted to give in to the erotically charged spell that she suspected he was capable of casting over her. If she let him.

But to do so was to dance with the devil, the devil being men who had no conscience or morals. She'd seen first-hand what such men could do to a woman. Okay, so maybe Jeremy wasn't as bad as her sister's abusive bully of a husband. Or that vile creep she'd gone out with from college. But he was still a serial womaniser who wanted a woman for one thing and one thing only. Admittedly, since meeting him, her own traitorous mind had been filled with that same thing. Clearly, Jeremy was a Casanova extraordinaire who didn't have to lift a finger to make women swoon. His elegant looks and his natural charm did it for him. And yes, that wonderfully sexy voice of his.

Despite being sorely tempted, Alice refused to become just another of this playboy's conquests. So she schooled her face into a polite smile before turning her head to answer him. Unfortunately, she hadn't anticipated just how close Jeremy's face was. Barely centimetres separated their noses, their eyes, their mouths...

Her smile froze in place as she stared at his lips, hating herself for wondering what it would be like to be kissed by them. But she wondered just the same. And she wanted. Oh, yes, she wanted. For a long moment she almost surrendered to the crazed urge to close the gap between them. But at the last second she pulled herself together. And he, thank God, leant back into his chair.

'I couldn't be a professional fund-raiser,' she said with her usual cool reserve. 'I don't like asking anyone for money. At least this way people get something in exchange for their donation. I've been assured the food and wine will be good, but of course there won't be much choice. It's a set menu, with only two dishes in each course, served alternatively so that people can swap if they want to. That's the only way the staff could cope with so many meals.'

'It looks good to me,' Jeremy remarked as the starters arrived at their table.

Alice was glad that she had something to concentrate on other than her crazy feelings. She glanced over at Jeremy's plate—scallops cooked in a white wine sauce—then down at her own, which was a stir-fried beef dish served on Asian greens. Alice heaved a sigh of relief when everyone at the table tucked in without swapping, all of them seemingly pleased with the food. And with the wine, red or white being offered by the constantly circling waiters. Each table already had jugs of iced water and freshly squeezed orange juice if people didn't drink alcohol. Mandy, who was on her right, chose the white, as did Alice. Not that she had any intention of drinking much.

'Eat up,' Jeremy said when she just sat there with her fork in her hand, and her mind still elsewhere. 'I love a woman who enjoys her food.'

Alice rolled her eyes at him. 'I get the impression that you love *all* women.'

He just smiled, not seeming in any way offended. 'You could be right there. They are definitely the nicer sex.'

'With the emphasis on the sex part,' she retorted, thinking to herself that she was insane to start this kind of tit-for-tat conversation.

He gave her a searching look. 'You don't like men much, do you? Or is it just me?'

Guilt consumed her at the realisation of how rude she had been when in truth he had done nothing wrong. Everything had been in her overheated imagination, plus her overheated libido.

'I do apologise,' she said sincerely. 'I'm not normally this rude. It's been a long and difficult day. I do like you. Honestly. I appreciate your coming tonight and being my auctioneer. It's just that...'

'What?'

She closed her eyes and shook her head. Impossible to explain the situation without being rude again.

'Nothing,' she added, opening her eyes and throwing him a wan smile. 'I'm a little tired.'

'You don't look tired,' he said. 'You look beautiful.'

Oh, Lord. He was like the Chinese water torture. 'Please don't,' she said with a low groan.

'Please don't what? Tell you that I think you're wonderful? I'd like to ask you out, Alice. To dinner, with me paying next time.'

Alice could not believe how tempted she was to just say yes. *Yes, yes, please take me out to dinner then take me back to bed.* It shocked her, the strength of that temptation, not to mention her desire. Fiona had been so right about Jeremy. He was seriously dangerous.

'Thank you for asking me,' she answered. 'I'm flattered. But my answer has to be no.'

His eyes narrowed as they scanned her face. 'Why is that, might I ask? You just said you liked me.'

'Do I have to give you a reason? Maybe I already have a boyfriend.'

'Do you?'

'No,' she said, lifting her glass of white wine to her lips. So much for her decision not to drink. But Lord, this man would drive any woman to drink.

'Girlfriend?'

Her startled gasp sent wine splashing over the rim of her glass.

With the speed of a quarter horse jumping out of the stalls, Jeremy whipped the snow-white handkerchief out of his breast pocket and dabbed at where the wine had run down her chin and throat, heading for her cleavage.

'Don't do that,' she snapped, even as her arms broke out into goosebumps.

'Don't be ridiculous,' he countered as he continued to mop up the wine.

Both George and Mandy said something but she wasn't listening, her focus solely on where that infernal handkerchief was straying, down towards her bullet-like nipples.

Just before he reached them, his hand stopped and he put the handkerchief away. Alice was not sure if she was relieved or disappointed.

'So what's your real reason for refusing to go out with me?' he asked her quietly as she snatched up her fork and attempted to finish her starter. 'And I'd like the truth, please.'

She swallowed one meagre mouthful before putting the fork down. 'If you must know, it's because of your reputation.'

He looked bemused. 'And what reputation is that?'

'Come now, Jeremy, you must know what people say about you. You're a playboy.'

'Oh, is that all?' he said, and laughed. 'And that's your only reason?'

She blinked at him. 'You don't think that's a good enough reason?'

'I've never come across it before.'

She just stared at him, thinking that she had never come across someone quite like him before, either. He was arrogant, yes, but with a wonderfully easy-going manner, which was both disarming and seriously seductive.

'I would imagine that not many women would say no to you, Jeremy,' she said truthfully. 'But I am. Please don't make a big deal about it. I'm not interested in wasting time on a man who thinks dating is a game and women are interchangeable.'

'I couldn't imagine ever thinking you were interchangeable, Alice. I can see that you are absolutely unique.'

'Why? Because I'm saying no to you?'

When he smiled she wanted to slap him. And kiss him. And say yes to him.

Her shoulders straightened as they did whenever life put her back against the wall.

'It's time for us to go auction off a few things,' she said coolly, and stood up.

CHAPTER SIX

By the end of the evening, Jeremy concluded that if he ever lost all his money and didn't want to return to banking he could become an auctioneer. Whipping up enthusiasm for the items on offer came naturally to him. But then, he'd always had the gift of the gab. He especially loved the thrill of the bidding wars, plus the moment when he brought the gavel down and said, 'Sold!' The whole process had been exciting. And profitable for the women's refuges. Alice seemed very pleased with the results. They had raised over four hundred thousand pounds from the auction alone, with the profit from the dinner lifting the total to half a million. Dear old George had contributed more than his fair share, bidding determinedly against a few other bidders for the privilege of having his name—plus his darling wife's—in Kenneth's next thriller. Mandy had been over the moon.

'I can hardly believe it,' Alice said afterwards. 'I never dreamt we'd raise so much. Of course, I have you to thank, Jeremy,' she added. 'You were brilliant.'

Jeremy didn't get too carried away with her compliment. There was still a wariness in her eyes during her dealings with him. Logic told him he was probably wasting his time pursuing Alice. But logic could not compete with the desire for her that had grown with each moment he spent in her company. She possessed a heady combination of mystery and allure, of unconscious warmth one moment and frosty reserve the next. It did irk Jeremy that, for the first time in his life, his reputation as a playboy wasn't working for him. It usually whetted female interest, most women wanting to see if he could live up to his reputation as a lover. Others obviously imagined that they would be the one to

ensnare his heart and make him settle down. They didn't
know they were fighting a lost cause. A few went out with
him just for fun. They were the ones he liked best.

Alice obviously wasn't any of those. She was a serious girl, with a serious outlook on life. He wondered if
her slightly anti-men attitude came from something that
had happened to her in the past, or maybe from where she
worked. It could hardly endear the opposite sex to Alice
if she was constantly dealing with women who'd suffered
from domestic or sexual abuse from their boyfriends or
husbands. He would never hurt her. He just wanted the opportunity to get to know her, and, yes, to get to *know* her.
Was that so wrong?

Yes, Jeremy, came a voice he wasn't used to hearing.
Possibly his conscience? *Alice is not the sort of girl who
could handle a fling with a man like you. You would probably end up hurting her, whether you meant to or not.*

Rubbish, another voice argued back immediately. His
male ego perhaps? *You're exactly what Alice needs. Dating
you will make her lighten up a bit. You can give her a fun
time, and pleasure. Lots and lots of pleasure!*

His loins prickled anew at this last thought.

Naturally, this second voice won the day, Jeremy refusing to be deterred despite Alice's earlier half-hearted rejection. She was attracted to him. He was sure of it. She just
had to get to know him better...

'I have some wealthy friends who would be only too
glad to make a substantial donation to your cause,' he said
as he accompanied her back to the foyer of the hotel. He
was thinking of Sergio and Alex, who were both generous
givers to charity, Alex especially. 'I'll give them a call tomorrow and get back to you. And then there's the matter
of my own personal donation.'

A startled Alice ground to a halt, throwing him what
could only be described as a panicky look. 'But I don't

expect you to donate a thing,' she said hurriedly. 'You've already been more than generous with your time tonight.'

'It was no hardship. I enjoyed every moment. But I didn't pay for my dinner. Neither did I buy anything at the auction. I can well afford to make a donation, Alice. I thought I might match what you raised tonight pound for pound. Now don't go thinking there any strings attached to this offer, because there aren't,' he continued before she could protest. 'So who will I send the money to?'

'What?' She seemed totally flustered.

'You have registered a proper charity, haven't you?'

'Yes, of course I have. It's called Save Our Refuges.'

'Right. I'll tell my friends.'

'The Bank of England is handling the donations for us. You can just transfer the money straight into the account. The details were on the email I sent to all the guests. But of course you weren't a guest, were you?' she added, frowning. 'I'll email Madge in the morning with all the information. But honestly, Jeremy, you don't have to donate that much money.'

'Why not? I can afford it. Besides, money doesn't go all that far these days. If you want to open more refuges you're going to need a lot more than a million pounds.'

'I suppose so…'

'Your charity will also need a few well-heeled patrons, like *moi*. You will need help, Alice, if you want to achieve the goals you set out in your speech. I'll tell you what, since you won't go out to dinner with me, why don't you drop by my office one day this week and we'll have a think tank on what other fund-raising activities you can employ? I'll see if Madge can join us. She's a smart lady and a fabulous organiser. I'm sure she'd love to be involved. How about Friday afternoon? Are you free then? If you're busy, we can make it next week some time.'

Alice still seemed reluctant, yet fiercely tempted at the same time. He could see a war going on in her eyes. But she would not, in the end, Jeremy believed, look such a gift horse in the mouth.

'I…well…yes, I suppose I can make it on Friday afternoon. But not till around four. Is that too late for you?'

'Not at all. Four would be fine.' Step one accomplished, which was to make her see that he wasn't such a bad guy. 'I'll have Madge email our address. Let her know if you can't make it and we'll reschedule.' Good to not sound desperate to see her again. Yet he *was* desperate. Weirdly, irrationally desperate. Jeremy could not envisage letting Alice just disappear from his life. He hadn't been this captivated by a woman in years. Or this challenged. She wasn't going to be an easy conquest. But, then, he didn't really want her to be a conquest. Despite his reputation as a ladies' man, Jeremy was not a rake, or a libertine. He genuinely liked women, liked their company, in bed as well as out. Seduction was not his usual game, possibly because he rarely had to employ such tactics. Getting a girl to go to bed with him had always been so damned easy.

Alice, however, was not going to be easy. Hell, he couldn't even get her to go out with him let alone go to bed with him. His pursuit of her was going to take patience, and some cunning. But he was sure she would be worth it.

His eyes ran over her one last time, imprinting her lovely face and figure in his memory bank so that he could download it into his mind at will during the next two days.

'I'll go get your coat,' he offered.

Alice could have told him that she would get it herself, but she knew that feminist defiance was useless against a man of Jeremy's nature. He might be a playboy, but he was also a gentleman of the old school who knew how to treat a woman. Alice felt both flattered and frustrated by his gallantry. She also felt flattered and frustrated by his determined pursuit of her. Clearly, he thought that making himself a patron of her charity would make her so grateful that she would finally agree to go out with him.

Silly man. She had no intention of doing so, despite the moments of sexual weakness, which he had effortlessly evoked in her tonight. But she would take his help, and his money, which was much needed by people who didn't have the resources or the resilience to help themselves. As she watched him walk over and collect her coat, she wondered if he had any idea at all what the women and children who fled to refuges had suffered. Or if he cared. Hard to imagine that a man of his wealth and background really cared about those less fortunate than himself. Or really cared about her, for that matter. She was just an attractive girl who'd dared to resist his charms and say no to him. She'd become a challenge, one which he smugly thought he'd eventually overcome. She'd seen the spark of triumph in his eyes when she'd agreed to come to his office on Friday.

Alice's mouth curved into a wry smile. If he thought she wasn't aware of his not very subtle ploy, then he was very much mistaken. Or maybe he didn't mind if she guessed how far he was prepared to go to get her, or how much he wanted her.

A shiver ran down Alice's spine at this last thought, a shiver that didn't bear too close an inspection. Because down deep, in that place reserved for unpalatable and somewhat scary truths, lay the fact that she secretly wanted him back. Perverse, really, given there was nothing to admire about Jeremy Barker-Whittle except his movie-star looks, his silver-tongued voice and his old-fashioned manners, all of which were either God-given or practised traits. He didn't show any genuine qualities that she could like and respect. Why, he'd actually *laughed* over his less than admirable reputation. What kind of man did that?

When he started walking back towards her with her coat draped elegantly over one arm, Alice steeled herself for what was to come next. She knew that if she put out her hand to take her coat he would ignore it. So she placed her purse and laptop down on a nearby armchair and waited till he got close enough before turning and lifting her arms away from her sides in expectation of his sliding the coat up them and over her shoulders. Which he did, oh, so smoothly, Alice despising the involuntary tremor that ran through her tensely held body.

'Where do you live?' he asked her as she struggled for total calm. 'Maybe we could share a taxi?'

What could she say? Silly to lie. 'I share a flat in Kensington,' she admitted as she picked up her laptop and purse.

By the time she glanced up at him, he was looking at her with surprised curiosity.

'That's where *I* live,' he said. 'In Kensington.'

'Really?' Was fate conspiring against her at every turn? She was trying to resist the man, not be thrown into his path each time. 'What a coincidence.'

'But a convenient one,' he said, smiling.

'Convenient?' she repeated somewhat archly.

'We should definitely share that taxi.'

'Well, yes, yes, I suppose so,' she said reluctantly.

Jeremy's sudden rise in temper startled him. Anger was not something he liked in others, or himself. He considered it poor form at the best of times. Only when severely provoked did he surrender to the temporary but often self-destructive comfort of fury. It had been many years since he'd lost it. Now that he thought about it, he hadn't truly lost his temper since his last year at boarding school when he'd come across one of the younger boys being bullied as he'd once been bullied. The fight that ensued had seen him almost expelled, only his father's paying for a new science block stopping that unfortunate event. Jeremy had rarely been grateful to his father for anything, but he was that day.

He'd really wanted to go on to university, and he might not have been accepted if he'd been expelled. Since then, Jeremy had steered well clear of all uncontrolled outbursts.

Occasionally, when annoyed with someone, he resorted to sarcasm. But that was as far as he usually went. The temptation to say something caustic to the ever reluctant Alice was acute, but counter-productive. So he simply smiled through clenched teeth and waved her ahead of him out towards the taxi station.

The ride from the hotel to her address in Kensington was blessedly short, with Alice sitting as far from him as possible with her knees pressed primly together, her laptop resting across her thighs, her head turned steadfastly towards the window. She didn't say a single word. Neither did he. Jeremy was half regretting his decision to pursue this girl. As intriguing as he found Alice, she wasn't worth losing any sleep over, or spending a small fortune on. His earlier assumption that she was attracted to him could be wrong. Either that, or she had some serious issues where the opposite sex was concerned. Maybe she'd been treated badly by a past boyfriend, some arrogant rich brute who'd cheated on her perhaps, leaving her bitter and cynical over men in general, and wealthy ones in particular. It would explain so much. Her chilly responses to his overtures. Her contempt of his reputation as a playboy.

By the time the cab pulled up outside her address, Jeremy felt confident that he'd hit on the reason behind her wariness where he was concerned. He couldn't have been wrong about her finding him attractive. No way.

'Thank you for tonight, Jeremy,' she said stiffly when she finally turned her head to look at him. 'You were a brilliant auctioneer, and a very pleasant dinner companion.'

He gazed deep into her eyes. 'Maybe we can do it again some time...' *But without the auction next time.*

Despite the dim light in the back of the cab, he saw the heat that suddenly flooded her cheeks, saw the startled widening of her eyes. Clearly, Alice was not used to blushing, wasn't used to having her composure rattled.

'We can discuss future auctions on Friday,' he added smoothly, his eyes still locked with hers.

'What? Oh, yes. Friday.' She seemed to have difficulty dragging her eyes away from his. Turning abruptly, she reached for the door handle before throwing an almost frightened glance over her shoulder. 'Please don't get out,' she said before he could do so. 'I'll see you at your office on Friday around four.' And she was gone, fleeing the cab with an unflattering speed, leaving Jeremy to smile ruefully at her ongoing resistance to the sexual chemistry that had just flared between them. Not just flared. It had fairly sizzled, with a heat that had left her flushed and him frustrated in a fiercely cruel fashion.

Jeremy watched her bolt up the stairs to the front door of her flat, the kind of flat that only rich girls lived in. She didn't turn back to wave at him before letting herself into the stylish town house. A light came on immediately, showing him that her flat was on the ground floor, which was always the most expensive. The upper floor and the basement flats would be cheaper. Though not much. Since investigating property prices in London more thoroughly, Jeremy knew that the most dilapidated flat in this area cost close to a million pounds.

He sat staring at the far from dilapidated town house for a few seconds before telling the driver to go on, his mind and his body in turmoil. It annoyed him that he hadn't found out a single personal detail about Alice tonight other than her lack of a boyfriend. He hadn't satisfied his rabid curiosity about her at all, let alone satisfied that other urgent need that had now arisen to torment him. Jeremy could not remember the last occasion he'd gone home alone after a date with a girl he liked. In actual fact, he couldn't recall that ever happening. Not that tonight was a proper date, he reassured his bruised male ego. Still, it rankled that for the first time in his life a girl had actually said no to him, especially one who he felt confident was sexually attracted to him.

By the time Jeremy exited the taxi in front of his stylish mews house three streets away, his resolve was firmly back in place, his ego refusing to accept her rejection. The bottom line was that he wanted Alice Waterhouse as he'd never wanted a girl before. And he meant to have her. End of story.

CHAPTER SEVEN

'NEW CLOTHES, I SEE?' Fiona said over breakfast on Friday morning, her tone very knowing.

Alice looked up from her bowl of oats, determined not to react to Fiona's continual niggling over her agreeing to Jeremy being a patron of her charity. 'Yes,' she said coolly. 'I hadn't bought anything new for ages and felt I couldn't show up at Jeremy's office in my old jeans and jacket. So I went shopping last night.'

'Your blouse is new too,' Fiona pointed out. 'And red. You never wear red.'

Alice shrugged. 'It was on sale and I liked it.'

'It's sexy.'

'Is it?'

'You know it is. So are those skinny jeans. He got to you, didn't he? I know you said you turned his dinner invitation down, but you and I both know, Alice, that he hasn't given up. His offering to be involved in your charity is just a means to an end. And you're the end.'

'I did find Jeremy attractive,' Alice admitted, privately thinking that that was the understatement of the year. 'But I still won't be going out with him.' Or so she kept telling herself. 'Look, the man is seriously rich, Fiona. It would be silly of me to cut off my nose to spite my face. If he wants to help with the charity then I'm going to let him. To refuse his support would be foolish. I don't know what you're so worried about. He's not that irresistible,' Alice added as she stood up and carried her unfinished bowl over to the sink.

'Huh. Tell that to the legions of women he's left frothing in his wake.'

Alice immediately thought of the over-made-up blonde

who would have dumped her partner on the spot if Jeremy had crooked his finger at her. The evidence of his charisma had been in her face all that night, the memory of his effect on her having stayed with Alice long after she'd fled their taxi. She could not deny that the thought of seeing him again today had inspired her shopping expedition last night. The red silk blouse *was* sexy, and hadn't been on sale.

'Want some more coffee?' she asked Fiona as she made herself some.

'Don't try to distract me with coffee, madam. I'm trying to talk some sense into you.'

Alice's patience with her friend finally ran out. Turning, she shot Fiona one of her chilly looks. 'I don't need anyone to talk sense into me, Fiona. I make my own decisions in life. Please stop warning me about Jeremy Barker-Whittle. If I ever change my mind and go out with him—and that's a big if, I can tell you—then it's no one's business but my own. Did I try to tell you not to become engaged to Alistair, despite his having the most irritating mother?'

Fiona looked a bit sheepish. 'She is irritating, isn't she?'

'Very. On top of that, what happened to your always telling me that I shouldn't be so down on men because of what just two of them did? You keep reassuring me that not all men are scoundrels. I'm beginning to think that maybe you're right. What harm would come if I had dinner with Jeremy? Or even if I went to bed with him?'

Fiona's big brown eyes rounded like saucers. 'You're thinking about going to bed with him?'

All the time, Alice thought. *Every minute of the day and night.*

'No,' she lied. 'I'm just saying it wouldn't be the end of the world.' Was it really her saying something so outrageous? So casual and carefree?

'But Jeremy *is* a scoundrel.'

'No, he's not,' Alice defended. 'He's actually very nice.

He's just a bit shallow, and spoilt. Inherited money doesn't do any man any good. But he's not nasty.'

'Oh, Lord. You're falling for him already.'

'Don't be ridiculous. I would never fall for a playboy. But he is fun to be around. I have to give him that.'

Fiona made a squawking sound. 'I don't know what to say!'

Alice had to laugh. 'Then don't say anything. Now I have to get to work. Are you going out tonight?'

'Alistair's taking me out for dinner. Some fancy French restaurant that's just opened in Soho.'

'Have fun, then. Talk to you tomorrow.'

Alice did her best to put aside thoughts of Jeremy on her way to work. Not easy when you were just walking or sitting, alone, on the Tube. Fiona's pointed comments this morning hadn't helped get the man out of her head. What had possessed her to defend him the way she had? Or to suggest that she might sleep with him at some time in the future? She knew she wouldn't. She couldn't. Aside from her ingrained distrust of the opposite sex, she was still a virgin, for pity's sake. A total ignoramus where actual sex was concerned. Jeremy would think she was some kind of weirdo if he ever found out.

By the time Alice got off the train at Hammersmith station, she'd determined to be polite and professional with Jeremy this afternoon. But she would not betray a hint of her inner feelings. If he flirted with her again, she wouldn't flirt back. If he asked her out again, she would definitely say no. Fiona had been right. He *was* a bit of a scoundrel; a man of manners but no morals. It was perverse how attractive she found him. But, then, life was perverse, wasn't it?

Alice sighed then headed for the refuge, which was in a four-bedroomed house located a few blocks from Hammersmith station. It was her favourite refuge to work in, a decent-sized place with a spacious back garden though somewhat run-down. They currently had half a dozen women staying there, along with several young children. The accommodation was cramped, but at least it was safe.

The house next door to them was still up for sale, Alice noted as she walked past. Nobody wanted to live next to a shelter, she supposed. But perhaps the charity could afford to buy it, if and when Jeremy's rich friends came through with some more donations. It would be interesting to see if he'd followed through on that. If he didn't, then she'd know that his so-called interest in helping out was nothing but a sham.

The thought dismayed her. She wanted him to be worthy of her liking him so much. Wanted him to prove Fiona wrong.

Well, she would find out the truth this afternoon, wouldn't she? Till then...

Alice steeled herself for the day ahead. Her job wasn't an easy one, most of the women she counselled too lacking in self-esteem to listen to what she was saying, let alone take her advice. But she did her best, which was all she could do. There were few easy solutions to the massive problems that faced society these days. Pasting a bright smile on her face, she let herself in the front door, almost immediately being confronted by two squealing children who were happily trying to kill each other. Girls, they were, possibly all of eight or nine.

Alice rolled her eyes as she grabbed the main aggressor by the back of her T-shirt, hauling her away from the other girl.

'Don't you think your mothers have enough problems without you two fighting and screaming like banshees?' she said firmly as she glowered down at both of them.

The girl she was holding pulled a face. 'What's a banshee?'

Alice prayed for composure. 'It's a ghost. A very scary ghost who wails at the walls whilst it haunts houses.'

'What's a wails?' the other girl asked.

Alice was very glad when their mothers appeared at the top of the stairs and called them away. Shaking her head after them, she walked slowly along the hallway and let herself into the room where she did her counselling. The sight of the mess in there showed that several of the children had been using it as a playroom overnight. Understandable, she supposed, given the lack of space, plus the fact that she did have some toys in there for the littlies who hated being separated from their mothers, even for a half-hour therapy session.

'Oh, dear,' Jane said from behind Alice's shoulder. Jane was the housekeeper and cook. A widow in her late fifties, she lived on the premises. 'Sorry about that.'

'It's all right,' Alice said, throwing the weary-looking woman a reassuring smile. 'It won't take me long to clean up.'

'You're a good girl,' Jane said, patting Alice on the shoulder before going off to do one of the million and one jobs she did in a day.

I try to be good, Alice thought as she started picking things up. *But I might not be so good after this afternoon's meeting with London's most infamous playboy.*

It was a troubling thought, yet at the same time an insidiously exciting one.

As Alice continued to clean up, her mind stayed on Jeremy. Was he really as good-looking as she remembered? And as charming? Would he ask her out again?

She hoped he would, at the same time hoping she'd have enough common sense to keep saying no. But Alice was beginning to doubt it.

He was a devil, all right. A wickedly sexy, almost irresistible devil!

CHAPTER EIGHT

'COME IN, MADGE,' Jeremy said at the sound of her familiar triple tap, a quick glance at the wall clock showing
that it was twelve minutes to four, a little early for Alice,
who he felt sure would keep him waiting, as she had the
other night.

Madge hurried in, holding a huge tome in her hands.

'I thought you might like to know a little bit more about
Alice,' she said in a conspiratorial tone, 'so I looked her up
in the latest *Who's Who.*'

'And?'

'She's the younger daughter of Richard William Waterhouse, the twenty-second Earl of Weymouth. Deceased,
it says. Her mother is Lily Amaryllis Waterhouse, nee
Knight. They had three children, Arthur William, who
died in childhood, then came Marigold Rose, followed by
Alice Hyacinth.'

'Someone has a thing for floral names,' Jeremy said
drily. 'Though Alice isn't a flower, is it?'

'Sweet Alice is. And I think there's a rose called Miss
Alice.'

'I see,' he said. 'Is that all it says about her?'

'Pretty well. Their ancestral home is called Hilltop
Manor, and is in Dorset, not far from Weymouth.'

Which wasn't all that far from his own family home in
Cornwall. Maybe he could offer to drive her down there
one weekend. Once she stopped playing Ice Princess and
decided to become a normal girl, that was.

'Thanks, Madge. That explains the voice but not the job.'

'You didn't find out much about her the other night,
did you?'

'Not much. She's not the kind of girl who would like being questioned.'

Madge's eyebrows lifted. 'Sounds intriguing.'

'That, she is. Very intriguing.'

'You like her, don't you?'

'Very much.'

'I thought you might. I mean, you're a generous man, but I wouldn't have thought that charity fund-raising on a regular basis is your thing.'

Jeremy had to smile. 'You know me too well, Madge. But personal issues aside, I do believe this is a very good cause. I would have wanted to help out regardless of how I felt about Alice.'

He noted how Madge's mouth twitched, as if she was having difficulty suppressing a smile. Or even a laugh.

'You've found me out,' he admitted. 'But for pity's sake, don't let the cat out of the bag when Alice is here. I'm trying to impress the girl, not make her even more wary of me.'

Madge looked taken aback. 'She's wary of you?'

'Either that or she's wary of all men. I asked her out and she said no.'

'No!'

'Yes. It was a definite no.'

'Maybe she already has a boyfriend.'

'She doesn't. She said so. She also said my reputation as a playboy had preceded me.'

'Oh, dear.'

Jeremy wasn't sure why he was telling Madge all this. There was nothing she could do. But it felt strangely comforting to have a sympathetic ear on the matter. He was no longer as confident of eventually bringing Alice round as he'd been the other night. Too much time had passed, filled with endless hours of doing what he hated doing. Thinking.

'I'd better get back to my desk,' Madge said. 'It's almost four.'

'When you bring Alice in, I want you to stay for a while, then I'll ask you to get us all coffee.'

Madge smiled. 'Okay.'

Alice broke her strict budget by taking a taxi to Mayfair. She hated wasting money, having spent the last few years saving madly for a flat of her own. She didn't care how small it was. She just wanted to own her own place. Hopefully, she would have enough by the time Fiona got married in August. She wouldn't, though, if she kept paying for cabs instead of taking the Tube. Still, this was a one-off...

Like buying new clothes the other night?

Guilt and excitement squirmed in her stomach as the cab turned down the street in Mayfair that housed Barker Books. It stopped outside a stylish white town house, which had a freshly painted black front door and colourful window boxes filled with flowers. After paying the driver, she climbed out and stood on the pavement for a full minute, scooping in several deep breaths in an effort to calm her galloping heart.

A young woman carrying two takeaway coffees hurried past her, running up the steps and elbowing the door open before stopping and throwing her a questioning look.

'Are you coming in here?' she asked.

'Yes,' Alice replied.

'The door's open,' the girl told her. 'It just swings shut sometimes. Who have you come to see?'

'Mr Barker-Whittle.'

'Right. Then you'll want to see Madge first. She's in the second room on your left.'

'Thanks.'

Sucking in one last gathering breath, Alice walked slowly up the steps and into the devil's lair.

Madge did her best to keep her expression neutral when Alice walked in. But she could see straight away what had captivated Jeremy. The girl was a delight to behold. Fresh faced and very pretty, with beautiful blue eyes, a cute nose and fashionably full lips. But whilst her clothes were modern and, yes, quite sexy, she wasn't wearing any make-up. On top of that, her blonde hair was pulled back into a girlish ponytail. Clearly, she'd made no effort to doll herself up for the occasion. Also clearly, she wasn't as enamoured of Jeremy as he was of her.

'You must be Alice,' Madge said as she stood up and walked around from behind her desk.

'And you must be Madge,' the girl returned with the sweetest smile. 'Thank you so much for all your help with the auction. Lord knows what I would have done if your boss hadn't put up his hand as auctioneer.'

'I gather he did a good job,' Madge said, then added drily, 'or so he informed me. Come, I'll take you to him.'

Alice's chest tightened as she followed Madge over to the heavy wooden door on which the PA knocked three times in rapid succession.

'Come in, Madge,' Jeremy called out, his deeply rich voice startling Alice anew. No man had a right to have such a voice as well as everything else. As Madge opened the door, Alice steeled herself to come face to face with his seductive physical presence, wondering not for the first time today why she was putting herself through such torture. It wasn't just to secure his patronage. The truth was she wanted to see him again. Silly Alice.

CHAPTER NINE

JEREMY'S OFFICE SHOULDN'T have surprised her. She'd already noted that the place hadn't been renovated in the modern style the way of a lot of London's town houses had been this past decade, stripping away all their old character-filled features in favour of soulless white walls and sleek lines, with recessed lighting and furniture that looked good but wasn't comfortable at all. Alice loved the wood-panelled walls, the glass-fronted bookcases, the polished wooden floor and the rather ancient patterned rug that sat in front of his antique desk.

Nothing was antique about Jeremy, however. He was all modern style, dressed in a dark blue suit, blue and white striped shirt and a flashy red tie.

'Alice is here,' Madge said on walking in.

'Excellent,' he replied, and rose immediately from behind his desk. 'So glad you could make it.'

He didn't look her over as he had the other night, Alice noted with a contrary degree of dismay, his eyes not on her at all as he placed a couple of straight-backed chairs right in front of his desk then returned to sit in his own black leather office chair.

'Sit down, ladies, and we'll get right to it.'

Alice and Madge sat down whilst Jeremy picked up a sheet of paper that had been lying on top of his desk.

'I've been giving the matter of further fund-raising some considerable thought,' he said, his eyes on the paper. 'I've jotted down a few ideas, which I'd like to run by you.'

Finally, he looked up, and their eyes met. No sparkling this time. No smiles. He was dead serious.

'Go on,' Alice said, despising herself for feeling so disappointed.

'First, we need to set up a website plus a social media page telling people about our aims and where they can send their donations. We can't just target the wealthy. Ordinary people making small donations are the mainstay of charities. Maybe you could see to that, Madge. You're good at that sort of thing.'

'Yes, I can set those up, no trouble.'

'Of course, after the success of the dinner and auction last Wednesday,' he went on, 'it's only sensible that we have another night like that. But not too soon. I thought perhaps in early December. It could have a Christmassy theme. What do you think, Alice?'

Alice had to force herself to focus. 'I think that's a marvellous idea,' she said with false brightness. 'We could decorate the ballroom and all the tables. And have a big Christmas tree on stage, with all the prizes under the tree in pretty boxes.'

'Sounds good. You'd better get onto booking that same hotel a.s.a.p. Christmas is a busy time. And I'll be paying for the decorations. You shouldn't have to pay for a thing, Alice. Professional fund-raisers always have expense accounts.'

'But I'm not a professional fund-raiser!' she protested.

'Maybe not, but you still shouldn't be out of pocket.'

Her laugh was dry. 'I'm not.'

'Thought that would be the case. Now *I'll* see to rustling up the prizes. I have lots of contacts and there's lots of time. Though feel free, either of you, to help in that regard. Now, Madge, if you don't mind, could you get me some coffee and biscuits? I missed out on having lunch today and I need some sustenance and a caffeine hit. What about you, Alice? Feel like some coffee? Or tea, if you prefer? Madge has everything in the kitchen.'

'Some coffee would be nice. White with two sugars.'

'That's a lot of sugar for someone so slim,' he remarked after Madge left. 'How do you manage it?'

Alice shrugged, having resigned herself to Jeremy's apparent loss of interest. 'I go for an hour's run every morning before breakfast.'

'I do so admire people who can do that. I have to confess I'm not a morning person. I hit the gym a few times a week in the evening but I'm not a dedicated exerciser. But you should still try to give up sugar, Alice. It's bad for you.'

She sighed. 'I know. I've tried but it's a habit I can't seem to break. When I was at boarding school they made great pots of tea with the milk and sugar already in it. After I left and started drinking coffee I found it way too bitter without the sugar.'

For the first time that afternoon his eyes showed some interest. 'You went to boarding school?'

'Yes.'

'For how long?'

'Seven years.'

'And did you like it?'

'I didn't mind it,' she said. Anything was better than being at home.

His blue eyes suddenly became bleak. 'I was sent to boarding school when I was eight, and I loathed it.'

Though her curiosity was sparked, Alice decided not to pry.

'Were you able to contact those rich friends of yours?' she asked instead. 'The ones who donate a lot to charities.'

'I sent both Alex and Sergio emails,' he told her. 'They might take a while to get to it, especially Alex. His wife's due to have a baby any minute now. He lives in Sydney. And Sergio lives in Italy.'

'Goodness. How did you get to be friends in the first place?'

'We all went to Oxford together.'

'I see,' she said thoughtfully. Not just handsome and rich and charming, but super intelligent too.

'You must have gone to university,' he said.

'No. I went to a college. At night. I studied psychology. I worked as a model during the day. Not a runway model. I wasn't tall enough for that. A photographic model, doing fashion shoots for brochures and magazines.'

'Well, you're certainly good-looking enough.'

The compliment was said so matter-of-factly that she took no pleasure in it.

'Did you like being a model?'

'It was okay. It paid the rent. But it wasn't what I wanted to do.'

'Did you always want to become a counsellor?'

'Yes, actually. I did.'

Jeremy wanted to question her some more but decided that might show too much interest. He'd decided to use reverse psychology today in an attempt to spark *her* interest. It was a tactic he'd seen other men use when in pursuit of a woman. He'd personally never had to go that far, but Alice was proving to be an elusive prey. Just take the way she looked today. Okay, the red blouse was marginally sexy, but mostly covered by a black jacket, as were her jeans. Her lack of make-up plus that girlish ponytail did not shout, *I want you to look at me, Jeremy. And I want you to want me.*

But for all that he did want her. More than ever. Wanted to tear through that cool façade of hers to the woman beneath. He'd seen glimpses of that woman and she was hot.

Jeremy winced as his thoughts sent messages south of the border, relieved when Madge came back into the room at that moment with a tray full of refreshments.

Alice wondered what had precipitated that odd look of distaste that had flashed across Jeremy's face. She suspected it had something to do with her. Maybe, on seeing her again, un-dolled-up this time, he'd lost interest in her. Maybe he now found her boring. Maybe his male ego was regretting going to all this trouble. Alice certainly regretted buying new clothes in some ridiculous need to look attractive for him. She'd planned on wearing some red lipstick to match the red blouse, and to leave her jacket off and her hair down as well; but, of course, her courage had failed her in the end.

Though maybe it wasn't a matter of courage failing her but common sense rising up to quell this ongoing urge she had to throw caution to the winds and do whatever he asked her. Which was insanity, pure and simple. She should be thankful that he'd lost interest, not depressed.

It took an effort of will to put aside her conflicted feelings for Jeremy and focus on what Madge was doing.

'What lovely mugs,' she said as she watched the woman pour coffee from an elegant silver coffee pot into three blue and white mugs.

'They're Spode,' Madge said. 'They were my mother's. The coffee pot was hers, too. She liked nice things. Two sugars, did you say?'

'Yes, please.'

Madge used some elegant silver tongs to drop two cubes into one of the mugs, then added some milk before stirring, then handing that mug over to Alice.

'Thank you,' she murmured politely.

'I'll leave the plate of biscuits on the tray,' Madge said. 'Feel free to help yourself.' And she went about pouring coffee into the two remaining mugs.

When Alice leant forward to select one of the cream biscuits, she glanced over at Jeremy, who wasn't looking at her face, but down at the rather deep V of her red blouse, definite hunger burning in his hot gaze. The startling realisation that he still desired her brought an instant heat to Alice's neck, her nipples tightening the way they had the other night. Her hand trembled, Alice having to take a firm grip of herself before she spilled hot coffee into her lap. Holding the handle tightly, she lifted it to her suddenly dry lips and took a small sip. Jeremy's eyes lifted at the same time, meeting hers over the rim of the mug. He didn't smile. Didn't blink. Just stared. And in that instant she knew, as surely as she knew white was white and black was black, that she wasn't going to be able to resist this man.

A dark stab of triumph rocketed through Jeremy when he saw the telling colour creep up from her chest to her throat, her very delicious throat, which was normally pale not pink, all her skin fair and clear and unlined. She was more innocent than his usual choice of woman. But maybe that was what entranced him. Maybe he'd grown tired of sleeping with women who'd been around the block too many times. He didn't doubt Alice had had lovers. No girl who'd been a model and been to college would have stayed untouched, despite that touch-me-not air she liked to adopt at times. But he suspected she hadn't had too many boyfriends. And he was sure that at least one of them—possibly the last one—had treated her badly. It was the only thing he could think of to explain her wariness where he was concerned.

But he could see that that wariness was lifting. Still, he would not rush things. Or her. There was something strangely exciting about taking his time to get to know Alice before he got to know her in the biblical sense. Not that he didn't think about that moment when she surrendered herself to him. Hell, he thought about it all the time. He was thinking about it now as he drank his coffee and tried to pretend he didn't have an erection as impressive as the Eiffel Tower.

The sound of someone knocking at his office door startled all of them, Madge jumping up from her chair.

'Go see who it is, Madge,' Jeremy told her.

It was Kenneth Jacobs, his ruddy face beaming at Madge, then at Jeremy as he was ushered into the office.

'Sorry to interrupt, Jeremy,' he said, his voice still a bit nasal from his cold. 'But I was passing by this way and just had to drop in and tell you how grateful I was for you stepping into my shoes the other night. It was very good of you. I hated letting that nice Alice down. I also wanted to say how pleased I am with what you've been doing with my books. Those new covers are perfectly splendid. I love them. And my sales speak for themselves. If you don't watch it, I'm going to be a rich man. Now I won't keep you. I can see you're having a meeting of some sort,' he added, throwing Alice a warm smile.

'Don't go,' Jeremy said, and Madge immediately got an extra chair. 'Stay and have coffee with us. And you can meet that nice Alice in person.' He waved a hand directly towards Alice.

Kenneth, despite being portly and almost bald and the wrong side of sixty, proved to be an incorrigible flirt, raining compliments on both Alice and Madge too, Jeremy noted—and insisting they call him Ken. He refused coffee. Instead he sat down and asked endless questions about the auction, pulling out a pen and notebook from his slightly crumpled cream linen jacket and jotting down George and Mandy's names, promising to give them major roles in his next book.

'I might make George the murderer,' he said with ghoulish glee, 'and his wife the victim.'

'Oh, no, don't do that,' Alice said straight away. 'Mandy will want to be in your book all the way through. Make Mandy the killer and George the victim. She could be a serial killer of husbands. A black widow.'

'I like the way you think, girl. That's a wonderful idea. Makes for a nice twist on the husband always murdering the wife.'

'I would imagine that quite a few wives might want to murder their husbands,' Alice said drily, and Ken laughed.

Jeremy didn't, however, the bitter undertone in Alice's words sounding personal, making him wonder which actual husband she was referring to. It came to him out of the blue that maybe she'd been married before. Briefly, but unhappily. That would explain a lot.

'Now when I was walking around Mayfair today,' Ken was saying. 'If you must know I didn't pass your establishment by accident, Jeremy. I was actually doing a bit of research for my latest book. Anyway, during my perambulatory travels, I came by this trendy little wine bar tucked away down the end of a cobblestone alley. It's called Pizza and Vino. There was something about it which called to me.'

Jeremy chuckled. 'Probably the irresistible smell that wafts from the place. They make the best pizza outside Italy. And the wine's not too bad, either.'

'I gather you've been there before, then?' Ken said.

'Yes. Once or twice.' Sergio had given him a taste for all things Italian. Plus he liked discreet little wine bars that had a relaxing ambience and were off the beaten track.

'I planned on returning later,' Ken said. 'Look, what say you call it a day, folks? Then we four could trot down there together for a few glasses of wine and some of that delicious pizza. Unless you have other plans, of course,' he added, shooting Jeremy and then Alice a rather intuitive glance.

Jeremy realised few people would be able to put much past Ken. Possibly, being a writer, he'd become a keen observer of life, and body language, and all sort of unspoken things.

Jeremy smiled, not worried a whit if his interest in Alice had been noted. Now that he was confident she returned his interest, his heart felt light, his mood very affable.

'No, no plans,' he said. 'Have you got plans, Madge?'

'None at all,' Madge returned, looking very pleased with the invitation.

'What about you, Alice?'

Her expression showed a degree of surprise, but no displeasure. 'No. No plans.'

'That's all settled, then.'

'I'll need to go to the ladies' room first,' Madge said, and stood up.

'Me too,' Alice said, and stood up also.

Ken chuckled. 'Women,' he said after they were alone. 'They do love going to the powder room in pairs. I wonder what it is they discuss in there.'

'Best we don't know, Ken. It's secret women's business.'

Jeremy had difficulty controlling his excitement when Alice finally returned with some glossy red lipstick on and her gorgeous blonde hair lying loose and wavy around her shoulders. Nothing could have pleased him more. Or aroused him more. Jeremy was glad that his suit jacket wasn't too short or too fitted, covering a good deal of his lower half. Whilst he no longer felt he had to hide his interest in Alice, he didn't want to frighten her off with the evidence of his lust. But already he was thinking she might agree to come back to his place tonight...

CHAPTER TEN

ALICE COULDN'T BELIEVE how much she liked just walking along the street with Jeremy. The pavement wasn't wide enough for the four of them to walk together so they'd broken off into pairs, Ken and a beaming Madge leading the way, she and Jeremy a few strides behind. He didn't make any attempt to hold her hand, for which Alice was grateful. She was already shaking inside. But with excitement, not fear. No, no, that wasn't entirely true. There was some fear mixed with the adrenaline racing through her veins, the same kind of fear which she imagined took possession of a first-time skydiver before he jumped out of a plane. Jeremy couldn't realise how new she was at this. Why, she hadn't been on a date since that last appalling time. Not that this was a proper date, she reminded herself. It had all come about by accident, not design, which was why she'd agreed. Because they wouldn't be alone.

Fiona would still be disgusted with her, of course. A part of Alice was disgusted with herself. What did she thinking she was playing at, encouraging Jeremy by wearing her hair down and putting on lipstick? Red lipstick, no less! Next thing she knew he'd be asking her out for real again. And next time, she just might not be able to say no.

He's a playboy, she kept telling herself. *An infamous playboy. And you're a virgin. You're not equipped to have an affair with a man like Jeremy. He'll eat you alive, then spit you out.* Because that was what playboys did. They took what they wanted, then they moved on.

She turned her head to glance over at him for the umpteenth time, thinking how utterly gorgeous he was. But, oh, so dangerous.

He turned his head towards her at the same time. 'What is it?' he asked, frowning.

Alice searched her mind for something sensible to say. 'I forgot to tell you something back at the office,' she said.

'What?'

'The house next door to the refuge I was working at today is for sale.'

'What's the price?'

'I don't know. I never envisaged we'd have the money to buy it.'

'Where exactly is this refuge?'

'In Hammersmith.'

'I see. And how big is this house?'

'Quite big, actually. Needs some work but I would say it has four bedrooms at least. And a big garden.'

'Then you probably don't have enough to buy it. Yet. But there's no harm in looking at it. Are you working to-morrow?'

'I always work on Saturdays. Friday nights invariably bring us a new client or two, looking for shelter from their drunken partners. By Saturday they're looking for an ex-cuse to go back to them and it's my job to talk them out of it.'

'Do you have much success?'

'Not enough. But I try.'

'I'm sure you're very good at what you do. You have a compassionate heart, Alice, nothing like the other girls I've known from privileged backgrounds.'

His comment startled her. 'What do you know about my background?'

'Nothing much. But I knew before you told me you went to boarding school that you came from an upper-crust fam-ily. Your voice gave you away, Alice.'

She sighed. 'I've tried to get rid of my posh accent, but it won't go away.'

'Don't try to change, lovely Alice. You're perfect as you are.'

She stopped and stared at him. 'Please don't say things like that.'

'Why?'

'Because you don't really mean it.' He was just saying it to get into her pants!

'Ah, but I do mean it, Alice.'

How sincere he sounded. How flatteringly, seductively sincere. He was a wicked devil, all right. But, oh, so charming, and disarming.

Alice had to laugh. It was the only way to defuse her tension and survive the evening.

'My answer is still no,' she said. And almost meant it.

Jeremy grinned then took her hand, giving it a light squeeze.

'You don't mean that,' he said. 'You're just playing hard to get.'

'I'm not playing at anything. *You're* the player, not me.'

'That old chestnut again? Now come along and stop being difficult. Besides, has it escaped your notice that I haven't asked you out again yet? So your no is premature. Or was that no referring to something else?'

Alice expelled an exasperated breath. 'You're incorrigible.'

'Too big a word. Almost as bad as perambulatory.'

Alice couldn't help it. She burst out laughing. Madge and Ken turned round to look at them.

'You two sound like you're having fun,' Ken said.

'We are,' Alice said in surprise.

Surprised that she was having fun with him? Jeremy wondered. Or that she was having fun, full stop!

Jeremy suspected both, the thought making him resolve to do everything in his power to make sure she had fun this evening. Maybe then she would stop saying no to his invitation to a dinner date. Just then Ken turned down the alley that led to the wine bar, Jeremy tightening his hold on Alice's hand as they followed.

'Watch your step,' he told her. 'Easy to trip on these old cobblestones.'

Pizza and Vino was a hit. Alice loved the look of the wine bar, which had subtle lighting, murals of Italian scenes on the walls and comfy semi-circular booths along the back walls. It wasn't all that busy yet, with pizzas not being served for another half-hour. They'd only just fired up the oven. Jeremy didn't mind that at all, ordering a couple of bottles of a superb Italian wine—one white and one red— hoping that that covered everyone's taste. Ken was happy to bow to his judgment, admitting that his knowledge of wine was limited.

'I'm normally a beer and Guinness man,' he said. 'Rather like my detective in my books. But I don't mind expanding my horizons,' he added, throwing Madge a rather flirtatious glance.

The next hour was extremely productive in Jeremy's quest to find out more about Alice, a couple of glasses of wine loosening up Alice's tongue, allowing him to probe a little without seeming obvious. It also helped that Ken was busy chatting up Madge. Jeremy soon discovered that the flat she was living in was owned by a girl called Fiona, an old school chum of hers and the younger sister of Melody, one of Jeremy's exes, Alice pointed out again. Though Lord knew he could hardly remember her. He vaguely recalled a Melody who was the daughter of Neville Drinkwater, one of England's richest stockbrokers. But he'd only taken her out once or twice. Spoiled society princesses never lasted long with him. Apparently her sister was nicer, having kindly given Alice a room for free when she'd first come to London after leaving school. This statement had led to some more questioning, Alice finally confessing that she didn't get along with her mother and didn't want to turn out like her.

'My mother cares for nothing but money,' she said as he refilled her glass a third time. 'She hasn't done an honest day's work in her life!'

Jeremy didn't admit that he already knew that she'd been born the daughter of an earl. No need to tell her that. Someone as naturally reserved as Alice wouldn't like to think he'd been prying into her background. He'd have to mention to Madge not to say anything. He glanced across their table at his PA. Dear Madge... She was having a wonderful time, talking books to Kenneth Jacobs. Unlike himself, she'd read every one of Ken's thrillers and was able to talk about each one in depth, much to the author's obvious pleasure. Jeremy couldn't say that those particular books were to his taste. Too grizzly. Too repetitive.

The waitress finally arrived with the pizzas they'd ordered, along with their mouth-watering smell. There was such an amazing array on the menu that in the end they'd opted for the house special, which had a little bit of everything.

'You were right, Ken,' Madge said. 'This looks delicious.'

'I agree,' Alice said. 'Thanks, Ken.'

Jealousy jabbed at Jeremy till Alice turned her lovely eyes his way and said sweetly, 'And thank you too, Jeremy. For the lovely wine. I know those bottles weren't cheap. And for everything else you're doing for my charity. You really are a nice man.'

It wasn't jealousy that stabbed at Jeremy then. It was guilt. Because none of today had been him being nice. It had been him being a ruthless bastard. Everything he'd done had had one purpose. To win Alice over and get her into his bed. And whilst he would be good to her—very good—just how long did he think their affair would last?

Not all that long, he conceded. He didn't do long. Or broken hearts, remember? Maybe he should just forget about Alice. She seemed the vulnerable type and he didn't want to hurt her.

If only she hadn't leant over at that moment and kissed him lightly on the cheek. He stared deep into her eyes and saw that they were glazed. Alice was obviously tipsy, every ounce of her usual wariness gone. In its place was a dreamy softness, plus the promise of what she would be like when she was naked and wide-eyed beneath him. It sealed her fate, that image. No way could he give up his pursuit of her. His need for her sharpened, a wry smile curving his mouth as he gave in to his dark side.

'I like your way of saying no,' he said, then leant over and kissed her back.

But not on her cheek. On her mouth.

Oh, Lord, Alice thought dazedly as his lips brushed over hers. Her heart started hammering behind her ribs, her stomach tightening, her head whirling.

His mouth abandoned hers way too soon, only then Alice becoming aware of Ken's chuckling, plus Madge's astonished stare.

'Yes, I fancy her,' Jeremy said with a smile in his voice. 'All right, Madge?'

Madge smiled. 'Quite all right with me, boss, if it's all right with her.'

'Is it all right with you, Alice?' Jeremy asked with that wicked sparkle in his eyes.

Embarrassment sent a hot blush to her cheeks, but some-how she found a cool voice. 'I will blame the wine for my lack of decorum, and Jeremy's male ego for his. I told him the other night that I wouldn't go out with him, but he sim-ply won't take no for an answer. Now I think we should eat our pizzas before they get cold.'

It was a struggle to keep her composure from that mo-ment on, her mind invariably returning to that moment when his lips had met hers. How could such a brief kiss give rise to such a storm of desire? She was awash with longing. And need. It underlined to Alice how dangerous it would be to go out with Jeremy, alone. She hoped and prayed that he wouldn't ask her again, and strangely, *annoyingly*, he didn't. Though after they'd finished their meal with coffee, he did suggest they share a taxi home. She agreed, assuming that all four of them would be in the taxi together, till Ken said that he and Madge were going in the opposite direction, to a jazz club Ken liked. To refuse Jeremy's offer at that point would have been silly. Besides, Alice didn't like catching the Tube at night, especially a Friday night.

The ride back to Kensington was just as short and as silent as their taxi ride the other night. It wasn't all that late. Only eight-thirty. She half expected him to ask her back to his place for a nightcap. But he didn't. He did, however, climb out of the cab when it stopped at her address, Jeremy telling the cabbie to wait for him. He walked her up the steps to her front door, turning her to face him before she could escape. Alice confessed privately that she wanted him to kiss her goodnight. In truth, she wanted so much more. Such wanting brought tension, and fear. She was out of her depth here with this man, sinking into waters that she wasn't equipped to handle.

'What are you afraid of, Alice?' he asked, frowning as his eyes searched hers.

'Maybe I'm afraid of myself,' she replied.

'You think too much. Time to just feel, Alice, and to have fun.'

'Fun?' she echoed. When had she ever had fun with a man?

He smiled. 'Clearly fun is a concept you're unfamiliar with. Let me teach you, Alice. I'm an expert at the art of fun.'

'I don't doubt it.'

'You're going to come to dinner with me tomorrow night, aren't you?'

Somehow, the word no simply would not come.

'Yes,' she said, sick of arguing with herself over this.

'Good. I'll ring you tomorrow and we'll make definite plans.' With that, he turned and left her, flushed and frustrated, on the doorstep. She watched him walk away and get into the cab without a backward glance. He did look at her through the taxi window but he didn't wave or smile. She thought he looked oddly grim, but maybe it was just her imagination. Why should he look unhappy over her agreeing to do what he'd been wanting her to do since Wednesday night? Which was say yes to him. Yes, to dinner and whatever else he had in mind for afterwards.

A shaken Alice let herself in the front door, glad that Fiona always stayed out late on a Friday night. She walked slowly along the hall and into her bedroom where she stripped off and dragged on one of her slightly prissy nighties. None of the outrageously sexy nightwear that Fiona always wore filled Alice's wardrobe. After a trip to the bathroom, she climbed into bed where she lay awake for hours, thinking about Jeremy, and tomorrow night, and fun.

By fun he obviously meant sex. Casual sex. Maybe even kinky sex.

Alice shuddered at this last thought. No way could she ever entertain the thought of doing anything remotely kinky. It was as much as she could handle thinking about having normal sex with him. Even whilst she wanted to, the idea of actually doing it at long last was overwhelmingly nerve-racking. How would he react when he found out she was a virgin?

Maybe he won't find out, Alice, came the comforting thought. *You've gone horse riding for years. And used tampons. You're not likely to bleed. Or feel excessive pain.*

Oh, Lord, she thought and buried her face in her pillow. *What have I done?*

* * *

Alice was still awake when Fiona got home just after one. Thankfully, her flatmate would still be asleep when she got up for work in the morning. Alice couldn't bear the recriminations over her spending the evening in Jeremy's company, then agreeing to have dinner with him. Fiona would be all dire warnings and doomsday forecasts. Silly, really. Alice knew full well there was no future with Jeremy. She wasn't a total fool. Not that she wanted a future with him, anyway. To entrust any man with her happiness forever was never going to happen. But she couldn't seem to stop herself from going out with him. He'd bewitched her—that was what he'd done.

As she lay there, Alice wondered if he was still awake, if he was thinking about her the way she was thinking about him. Hardly, she decided cynically. Playboys didn't lose sleep over members of the opposite sex. She suspected that if a woman gave Jeremy cause for trouble, he simply shrugged her off and moved on. Clearly, that was what he'd done with Melody. Sex was a game to him. Women were rest and recreation. He didn't have relationships. He had fun. Girlfriends weren't permanent fixtures in his life. They were never proper girlfriends at all. They were just dates. Any woman foolish enough to go out with him had to accept that. Alice had already accepted it because, quite frankly, his way of life suited her. That didn't mean dating him didn't frighten the life out of her. It did. But there was no going back now. She was well past the point of no return...

Jeremy threw back the duvet, jumped out of bed and stalked, naked, from his bedroom along the hallway and down the stairs into his den. A typical man cave, it had everything he needed to entertain himself at home. A billiard table, a huge TV on the wall, games console, a large comfy sofa, an armchair near a bookcase full of complex spy thrillers, plus a well-stocked bar. Whilst Jeremy was a wine buff, when he was attacked by insomnia his mainstay was whisky. Pouring himself a hefty slug, he sipped it straight as he sank into the sofa and picked up the remote. But then he dropped it again. He didn't want to watch TV. He wanted to be in bed with Alice.

Damn the woman. She'd really got under his skin, hadn't she?

He knew why. Because she was different from the women he usually dated. Underneath that cool façade she hid behind, she was sweeter. Nicer. And sexier in a weirdly innocent way.

The look on her face when he'd left her on the doorstep, unkissed, had made him feel rotten. But he'd done it, anyway. Because he'd wanted her to go to bed wanting him.

Jeremy laughed, aware that his cold-blooded plan had backfired on him. He was the one left doing the wanting. Hell, he wanted her so badly that he couldn't sleep. She, no doubt, was already racking up zeds, whilst he was here, with a painful hard-on, drinking himself into oblivion. He took comfort from the fact that tomorrow would come. And so would tomorrow night. He wouldn't be leaving her unkissed tomorrow night, he vowed. There wouldn't be an inch of her delicious body unkissed.

Jeremy smiled a dark smile as he gulped back some more Scotch.

Just you wait, Alice. Just you wait.

CHAPTER ELEVEN

LUCKILY ENOUGH, NO new clients had arrived at the shelter on the Friday night, which meant that Alice's lack of concentration that Saturday wasn't obvious. She spent the morning talking to a few of the women who'd been there a while, encouraging one of them to go home to her parents, who had agreed to help. But she was too afraid of her ex showing up and making trouble. She had no confidence in the restraining order she'd taken out against him. No confidence in the police doing anything but smacking him on the wrist.

By the time Alice stopped to make some coffee to go with her sandwich for lunch, she felt decidedly weary. Not enough sleep, of course. On top of that, Jeremy hadn't rung. She wished he would put her out of her misery and just ring.

As if she had conjured him up by sheer wish power, her phone rang, and it was him, just the sound of his voice instantly dispelling her tiredness, in its place a fizz of excitement, and anticipation.

'How's my girl today?' he said.

'You are a terrible flirt,' she replied, but with a smile on her face. 'But you know that, don't you?'

'It's been mentioned once or twice. So would it be all right if I came over and we had a look at the house next door together some time this afternoon?'

'Oh. Oh, yes, I suppose so,' she said, thinking she didn't look as smart as she had yesterday. The jeans were the same but her top was a simple and rather cheap white T-shirt. The weather had turned warm, so a jacket was out of the question. She wondered if she'd have time to dash down the road and buy something new.

'What time were you thinking of coming?'

'Have no idea. When would you suggest?'

'Not for a couple of hours. I've got appointments,' she lied.

'Tell you what. If you give me the name of the estate agent handling the sale, I'll give them a call and arrange a proper inspection. How about three?'

'But what if he can't organise things that quickly? That's not much notice.'

Jeremy laughed. 'Trust me, Alice, the agent will drop everything to show me that house at three. Money speaks all languages, but especially that of greed. Now go get me a name. And you'd also better tell me your work address. I only know Hammersmith.'

After she told him everything he needed to know, she added that it would be better if she met him at the house rather than the refuge.

'Why's that?' he asked in a puzzled tone.

'There are lots of nervous women here, Jeremy,' she informed him. 'And you're a strange man. Sorry. No offence intended.'

'None taken,' he replied. 'Okay, we'll meet outside the house for sale at three.'

'Fine,' Alice agreed. 'Ring me if you can't make it. Bye.' And she hung up. Alice bypassed the coffee, stuffing the sandwich down her throat before telling Jane she was off up the road to do some shopping. One hour later she was the proud owner of a very nice floral blouse—floral was in this spring—along with an off-white shirt dress, which was simple yet stylish enough to take her to whatever restaurant he took her to tonight. Alice loved the way it gave her a very feminine shape, being cinched in at the waist with a wide self-covered belt. The buttons—which ran all the way from the V neckline to the hem—were gold, but small and dainty. She also splurged on a pair of nude high-heeled sandals. This was followed by a matching clutch purse, bringing the bill to more than she'd spent on clothes in years. Her final purchase before returning to work was a coral lipstick, bought on impulse as she walked past a shop that sold make-up.

Alice knew she was acting unwisely—everything she'd done since meeting Jeremy had been unwise—but there was no stopping now. But underneath her surface excitement, she was anxious.

As the clock ticked closer to three she started constantly popping her head out of the front door, checking to see if Jeremy had arrived. He'd be late for sure. Maybe he wouldn't come at all. She half expected her phone to ring, calling his visit off. By the time a silver Aston Martin pulled into the small off-street parking area in front of the house, Alice was in a right old state. She swallowed as she watched a dashingly attired Jeremy climb out from behind the wheel. God, but he was gorgeous, that pale grey suit he was wearing decidedly yummy. He was yummy all over, she conceded breathlessly as she quickly closed the door lest he see her ogling him again.

'Just popping out for a short while,' she called out to Jane, after which she took several deep breaths and tried to gain control of her silly self. Pride demanded she not let Jeremy know how much he was affecting her. Pride and common sense. If he suspected how crazy she was about him, he'd go in for the kill. Tonight. Alice needed more time before going to bed with him. She wasn't remotely as unconcerned about doing such a thing as she'd intimated to Fiona that other morning. Jeremy might think of sex as just fun, but for Alice to trust a man with her body was a huge leap of faith for her. A huge decision, and not one she aimed to make lightly.

'Hi there,' she said as she walked with feigned serenity towards him. 'You're very punctual,' she added.

Oh, the irony of that remark, Jeremy thought as he looked Alice up and down. If there was one thing he'd never been in his life, it was punctual. He'd improved a bit after buying his own business, but since meeting Alice he was in danger of becoming an obsessive clock-watcher. Waiting till lunchtime before ringing her today had been agony. He'd been tempted to come early this afternoon as well, but in the end had practised patience, instinctively knowing that rushing Alice in any way, shape or form would not work. At the same time, he hadn't expected to be greeted by cool blue eyes, showing him that *she* hadn't been on tenterhooks waiting for him to arrive.

Never had he known a girl run so hot and cold all the time! The thought that her co-operative behaviour last night had been due to her being drunk did not sit well with Jeremy. He much preferred to think that she'd finally fallen victim to the same uncontrollable desires that were currently gripping him. It was one step forwards and two steps backwards with her, he conceded.

Damn it, but she was lovely. He found more features to admire every time he looked at her. Her small shell-like ears. Her daintily pointed chin. Her clear, almost translucent skin. But always at the centre of his attention was that luscious mouth.

The temptation to grab her and kiss her senseless was acute, and most uncharacteristic of him. Jeremy never made love to a woman like some caveman. He never grabbed. He caressed. He never insisted. He persuaded.

'The owners are away in Spain so the place is empty. The chap handling the sale said we could inspect it at our leisure.'

The house proved to be in surprisingly good condition for a building as old as it was. The kitchen and two bathrooms had been renovated at some stage, and the walls freshly painted, though a lot of the Victorian features had been maintained, with the two reception rooms still having their original fireplaces and lovely ornate ceilings. There were four bedrooms, plus another small room, which was being used as a study. Of course the price was prohibitive, the million they'd raised not enough to purchase it. When Alice mentioned this, Jeremy turned to her.

'If you like I'll buy it and gift it to your charity.'

A shocked Alice blinked in amazement. 'That's too much, Jeremy. I can't let you do that.'

'Why not?'

'You know why not.'

He shook his head at her. 'My dear, cynical Alice, you're quite wrong. I would never go that far just to get a girl to go to bed with me. I genuinely want to help. I was touched by your speech the night of the auction. And I found the reason why I shouldn't just rock up at the refuge door quite heartbreaking. I feel genuinely sorry for all those poor women. I admit my offering to get more involved in your charity wasn't entirely altruistic at first,' he went on, that bewitching sparkle lighting up his eyes. 'Yes, I confess I wanted to see more of you and I thought you wouldn't give me the chance. But last night changed my game plan. You agreed to go to dinner with me tonight so you see I don't need to do this. I *want* to do it, Alice. I can easily afford it.'

Alice just stared at him, his words revolving in her head, especially his confession of having a 'game plan'. She'd suspected from the beginning that his offer to become a patron of her charity had been a ploy. Fiona had warned her that he was a devil when it came to women.

'Just how rich are you?' she threw at him in an effort to remind herself just who she was tangling with here. An infamous playboy. A man who thought of sex as a game. His needing a *game plan* in his pursuit of her had been very telling. She wished she didn't also find that thought secretly exciting, and perversely flattering.

He laughed. 'I don't usually tell women the extent of my wealth. But in the interest of putting your mind at rest I have a couple of billion at my disposal.'

Alice gasped. 'A couple of *billion*?'

'Yes.'

'Good Lord.'

'I have been lucky.'

'Lucky how?' she quizzed, shocked. He didn't seem old enough to have accrued so much money. He didn't look any older than thirty.

His shrug was nonchalant. 'I did inherit some of it. But the rest I earned myself. Plus an investment I made in my early twenties, which paid off big time last year.'

'What kind of investment?' She was both curious and intrigued.

'I'll tell you about it over dinner tonight. Right now there's something else I'd rather do…'

Alice knew he was going to kiss her well before he drew her into his arms and lowered his mouth to hers. She could have said no. Could have made some silly futile protest. But it wouldn't have been honest. She wanted him to kiss her. And not the light brushing of lips he'd given her last night. She wanted a more passionate display of his desire.

Be careful of what you wish for, Alice…

His kiss was soft at first. Almost gentle, his arms around her not threatening in any way. He teased her lips open, slowly, seductively. But once he gained entrance to her mouth, the tenor of his kiss changed. His arms tightened around her, his tongue delving deep, making her gasp as white-hot lights exploded in her brain. She couldn't get enough of him, her own arms sliding under his suit jacket to wind around him, clinging wildly to his firm, hard body. She moaned as fire flooded her own body, burning her up with a longing that was as powerful as it was wonderful.

When his phone rang, she groaned with dismay. He ignored it for a couple of rings, but then his head lifted, his eyes looking oddly stunned.

'Wow, Alice. What happened to my Ice Princess? Sorry, but I need to answer this.'

CHAPTER TWELVE

JEREMY KNEW HE didn't need to do any such thing. He wasn't expecting a call. He could have just ignored it. It would have gone to his voicemail eventually. The truth was he'd been close to losing control. Not a good idea when you were without a condom. He usually kept a couple in his wallet, but had run out recently. He'd bought a new box the other day, then forgot to open it. Which showed how crazy Alice had been making him.

He wouldn't be forgetting them tonight, he vowed darkly as he checked the identity of his caller. It was Sergio, possibly getting back to him over the email he'd sent concerning Alice's charity.

'Sergio,' he answered, throwing a flushed Alice an apologetic smile. Lord, but she looked even lovelier when she was hot and bothered. Now that he knew she wouldn't knock him back, tonight could not come soon enough. 'What are you up to, dear friend? I presume you got my email?'

'Email?' Sergio echoed, sounding confused for a second. 'Oh, yes, about the charity. I've already wired off a donation. Was half a mil enough?'

'Perfect.'

'That's not why I'm calling.'

'Oh? What's up?'

'The premiere of *An Angel in New York* is on in a fortnight's time. It's in New York, of course. I thought since you were one of the executive producers that you might like to come. Sorry I didn't invite you sooner but things have been up in the air with the release date for some time. Last-minute editing and all that. Anyway, I invited Alex as well, since he also put money into the movie, but with Harriet due any day now he refuses to travel.'

'Fair enough. But I'd love to come.'

'You can stay with us at Bella's New York apartment.'

'No, I wouldn't want to impose. Besides, I'll be bringing someone with me, if that's all right.'

'Of course. Who is she? Someone new?'

'Yes. Her name's Alice,' he said, glancing over at Alice, who was looking a little less flustered. 'She's the girl who started up the charity. She's a counsellor. Works for the women's refuges.'

'Sounds intriguing. And not your usual type.'

'Right on both counts.'

'Dare we hope you've fallen in love at long last?'

The question startled Jeremy, then annoyed him. Surely Sergio knew him well enough by now to know that was never going to happen. 'Don't be ridiculous.'

Sergio sighed. 'I don't think falling in love is ridiculous.'

'You're entitled to your opinion. But then, you're biased.' No doubt Sergio believed he was genuinely in love with Bella. Romantic love was an illusion, in Jeremy's opinion. A mirage. Get close enough and it disappeared. Liking and lust, however, were very real and more stable emotions. He liked Alice and he lusted after her. He had not, however, fallen in love with her. Jeremy knew from experience that love made men do seriously stupid things, like get engaged and vow eternal devotion. He didn't want to propose marriage to Alice. He just wanted her to go out with him, and go to bed with him.

'I didn't ring you to argue about love, Jeremy,' Sergio said, his stiff tone making Jeremy feel ashamed of himself. He had no right to spoil what was no doubt a happy time for Sergio. He should let him enjoy his marriage and his wife, whilst the gloss lasted.

'Sorry,' he said. 'I'm an old cynic, I know. Look, I'm a

bit busy right now. Could you send me the details of the premiere and I'll book a hotel?'

'Will do. We'll talk again soon. Keep well.'

'One of your old friends from Oxford?' Alice said after he put his phone away.

'Yes. Sergio's one of the main reasons I'm a billionaire. Plus why I'm addicted to Italian food. He and my Australian friend, Alex, were the instigators of the investment which reaped in all the money. They did most of the work. I was just the behind-the-scene money man.' He considered telling her more about the WOW bar franchise, then decided Alice didn't need to know the ins and outs of his past life. He'd found that telling a woman too much about himself gave her the impression you wanted more from her than what he was capable of giving. He was already in danger of giving Alice the wrong impression by becoming involved in her charity. Still, he did like talking to her. A lot. Hell, but he was damned if he did and damned if he didn't!

'From what George said the other night,' she said thoughtfully, 'you're a very clever man with money.'

Jeremy shrugged off his momentary emotional dilemma, determined not to go getting too serious here. Life was meant to be enjoyed, not fretted over. 'That I am,' he said.

'And with women,' she added pointedly.

'I do have talents in that area also.'

'You *are* incorrigible.'

'And you're a very good kisser.'

Alice had to laugh. If only he knew...

'What was that all about you bringing me along somewhere?'

'Sergio's wife has made a movie which is premiering in New York in a fortnight's time. It's called *An Angel in New York*. As one of the executive producers, I've been invited. I thought you might like to come with me.'

Her eyes widened. 'To New York?'

'Yes. What do you think?'

'I think you're very presumptuous,' she said. 'Is Sergio's wife a famous actress?'

'Bella? No, not really. She's a Broadway star.'

Alice gaped. 'What? You're talking about Bella? *The* Bella?'

'The one and only.'

'Oh, dear. Oh, you wicked man!'

'Why?'

'I saw her once, on stage, in London. She's simply brilliant and so beautiful. I would kill to be at the premiere of that movie.'

'Well, you don't have to kill anyone, Alice. Just buy yourself a nice new dress and come along with me.'

'Like I said, you're a wicked man.'

His smile made her melt inside, but she maintained her droll expression. 'I don't have money to burn, Jeremy. I am saving to buy my own flat. If I come with you—and I haven't said yes yet—I will wear the same outfit I wore to the charity auction the other night.'

'Fine,' he agreed equably. 'You looked great in that.'

'Now I have to get back to work,' she said before he could kiss her again.

'Fine,' he repeated, though through gritted teeth.

'What time are you going to pick me up tonight?' she asked him as they made their way outside.

'How about seven-thirty?' he suggested after locking up.

'Could we make it eight-thirty? Fiona will have gone out by then.'

He frowned. 'What's going on here, Alice? Why the cloak and dagger stuff? Are you ashamed of going out with me?'

'I'm not going out with you. I'm just going to dinner with you.'

'I see,' he bit out. 'In that case, we'll stick to seven-thirty. I don't like to eat late. But I'm disappointed in you,

Alice. I thought you were a girl who knew her own mind. And who didn't let other people influence you. You don't have to answer to your flatmate. You're a grown woman, without a husband, fiancé or boyfriend. You don't have to answer to anyone.'

Alice swallowed. He was right. She didn't. But there were times when she needed a shoulder to cry on, or some advice from others. It was hard not having a mother you could rely upon, or a big sister with any sense. Fiona might not be the sharpest tool in the box but she had Alice's best interests at heart, unlike the man standing in front of her. He didn't have her best interests at heart at all.

'Seven-thirty it is, then,' she said somewhat coldly.

'Oh, Alice, Alice,' he said, shaking his head at her. 'Whatever am I going to do with you?'

'You're going to take me to a very nice restaurant to-night,' she retorted with defiance in her eyes. 'And you're going to tell me how you came to be a billionaire.'

He stared at her for a long moment, then smiled. He was still smiling as he climbed behind the wheel of the sleek silver Aston Martin, which had playboy written all over it.

Alice watched him reverse out into the street, then roar off, her stomach tight with tension over the night ahead.

'Oh, Alice, Alice,' she muttered to herself as she turned and walked slowly back to work. 'Whatever *is* he going to do to you?'

CHAPTER THIRTEEN

As LUCK WOULD have it, Fiona wasn't there when Alice arrived home from work around six. She'd left a note propped up on the hall table, informing Alice that she'd gone to Alistair's place, and wouldn't be home till late. Relieved, Alice dashed to her bedroom, dropping her things on the bed before hurrying into the bathroom and turning on the taps of the claw-footed bath. She only had an hour and a half before Jeremy picked her up and there was so much to do...

Jeremy pulled in to the kerb outside Alice's flat right on seven twenty-nine, taking his time as he alighted the car, locked it then walked slowly up the steps to the front door. Scooping in a deep breath—Lord, anyone would think he was nervous!—he pressed the buzzer and waited impatiently for someone to answer, all the while wondering which Alice he was going to be taking out tonight. The hot babe who'd kissed him back so passionately this afternoon, or the Ice Princess whom he'd first met and who bobbed up with regular monotony. She was a mystery all right. Irritating and intriguing yet downright irresistible. He hadn't been this excited over a date in years.

The door opened and there she stood, the Ice Princess, in a prissy cream dress and her hair all scraped back into that bun thing. Not that she didn't still look beautiful. She did. But truly!

'You're early,' were her first words, served cold in that cut-glass voice of hers.

Jeremy didn't wear a watch, so he pulled out his phone and showed her the time.

'Oh,' she said. 'I must have lost track of time. I'll just get my bag.'

When she whirled round and walked back into the hallway, the softly falling skirt of her dress flared out slightly. Jeremy's gaze dropped down to her shapely calves, and then down to her very sexy shoes. It came to him, when she walked back towards him with her bag tucked under her arm and keys in her hand, that the dress wasn't quite as prissy as he'd originally thought. He liked the way the buttons went from the neckline to the hem, his mind already anticipating the ease with which he could undress her.

'You look lovely,' he complimented as she locked up. 'I like that dress.'

'Do you?' She sounded uncertain. 'I liked it when I first bought it but when I put it on tonight I wondered if it was a bit old-fashioned.'

'It suits you,' he said.

'Thank you,' she replied stiffly before heading down the steps ahead of him, her shoulders squared as if she were going to face the firing squad.

Jeremy suppressed a sigh, saying nothing whilst he opened the passenger door for her, waiting till she was buckled up before he closed the door and made his way round to the driver's side.

'Is there anything wrong, Alice?' he asked her once he was behind the wheel. 'Did your flatmate make some more derogatory comments about me? What was her name again?'

'Fiona. And, no, she didn't say a single word about you. She wasn't at home. She'd gone over to her fiancé's place.'

'Then what's bothering you?'

Alice winced before turning to throw him a small, apologetic smile. 'To coin an old cliché, Jeremy: it's not you. It's me.'

'Want to talk about it?'

'No. No. Not yet. I'll sort myself out. Let's just have a nice night out.'

'That won't happen unless you relax, Alice.'

Her smile turned rueful. 'Perhaps after a couple of glasses of wine, I'll do just that.'

Jeremy frowned. He didn't want her drunk. He wanted her well aware of who was making love to her later tonight. Which would be him, Jeremy Barker-Whittle. More than ever before, he suspected that some man in her past had done her wrong. And he was suffering for it.

'Do you mind if I ask you one question before we go?'

'What?'

'Have you ever been married?'

The look on her face gave him his answer.

'No. Right. My mistake. Just thought it might explain why you're so wary of men. A bad marriage can be very damaging. I know. My family's littered with bad marriages. The number of divorces they've accrued between them must be some sort of record.'

Alice heard the bitterness in Jeremy's voice, a most unusual occurrence. He was usually so easy-going, so carefree in his attitude to life.

'Like...how many divorces?' she asked.

Jeremy laughed as he gunned the engine. 'Let's see now... Dear old Dad's on his fourth marriage. Mother's got three divorces behind her. Fortunately, she hasn't married her current partner, which is a bonus since I hear that's already on the rocks. My oldest brother, Winston, is about to enter his third marriage whilst my other brother, Sebastian, is really letting the side down. He's only on his second marriage.'

'Goodness. That is a lot of divorcing.'

'Tell me about it,' he said as he drove off. 'And they wonder why I've chosen a different path in life. I decided a long time ago to remain a bachelor.'

'Understandable,' she said. And she *did* understand. 'We are all products of what happens in our families,' she went on, thinking of her father's suicide plus her mother's blind materialism. Alice blamed her entirely for Marigold sticking with her abusive husband, just because he was rich. 'It's impossible to remain unaffected by our parents' mistakes. In an ideal world, they should be role models. But real life doesn't always work out that way.'

Jeremy flashed her a surprised glance. 'I keep forgetting that you studied psychology. But let's not talk about such matters tonight. At the risk of disappointing you by eating Italian two nights in a row, I'm taking you to my favourite Italian restaurant where we're going to eat some seriously good food, washed down with some seriously good wine.'

'And afterwards?' Alice asked before she could think better of it.

His shrug seemed nonchalant. 'Afterwards will be up to you. I can either take you straight home, or you can come back to my place for a while.'

'Where we would do what, exactly?'

He smiled over at her. 'Have some seriously good sex.'

A highly charged shiver ran down Alice's spine. Oh, Lord, she'd walked right into that one, hadn't she?

'Do you always have sex at the end of a dinner date?' she asked with feigned calm.

'Pretty well. Don't you?'

'I haven't had many dinner dates lately.'

'Or any dates at all, I'm beginning to suspect.'

'No...'

'Why not?'

Alice wasn't ready to tell him the total truth. She'd already decided to go to bed with him tonight. It was time. And he was ideal, a handsome, experienced lover with an irresistible sex appeal. On top of that, she *trusted* him. A perfect first lover for her, in every way.

'Why not, Alice?' he persisted.

She could see that she had to tell him something.

'I had a bad experience with a date a little while back.' To say five years would have sounded neurotic. Which she was, of course. Alice understood her own emotional baggage very well. But understanding did not always bring change. Her decision to go to bed with Jeremy tonight was a huge change for her. A huge decision. It was also the reason for the crippling tension that had gripped her when she'd met him at the house earlier, making her freeze up when she saw him standing there; a real man, not some fantasy figure.

Jeremy was shaking his head. 'My God, Alice, are we talking date rape here?'

Alice swallowed. 'Close to.'

The shock—and the sympathy—on Jeremy's face was strangely soothing.

'That's terrible, Alice. Simply terrible. You must have been horribly upset. Did he hurt you?'

'Not physically. I managed to get away before he could actually do the deed.'

Maybe not physically, Jeremy thought. But the emotional damage had been enormous. It explained a lot about Alice. Her distrust of men. Her wariness with him. He'd bet London to a brick on that her assaulter had been rich, and arrogant, and not used to taking no for an answer.

A bit like you, Jeremy, that annoying voice piped up.

I'm nothing like that, he argued back. *Not even remotely.*

Still, he realised he would have to take things carefully with Alice.

'I thought something bad must have happened to you to make you so wary of the opposite sex,' he said gently. 'But you can't let one man taint your view of all of us, Alice. I would never force myself on any woman. I respect them too much for that. My mother might be a fool when it comes to relationships but she's a lady who taught me how to treat a lady. If there's one thing I'm grateful to her for it's that she brought me up to have manners.'

But no morals, Alice almost said, just biting her tongue in time.

'I can see that you're a gentleman, Jeremy,' she said instead. 'Otherwise I wouldn't be here with you.'

'Good. Glad we got that straight. We're here,' he announced, pulling his car off the road and driving down a narrow side street into a small back car park, which was almost full.

The restaurant was nothing like she expected. Not very Italian in decor, it had a distinctly Bohemian atmosphere, its maître d' a redhead of around forty who eyed her up and down with the kind of look Alice imagined an ex-girlfriend would employ. Very droll, as though wondering what on earth Jeremy saw in her.

Her smiles were all for Jeremy as she escorted them upstairs to a table tucked away in a very private corner.

'Our special tonight is mussels,' she informed them once they were seated, 'cooked in a delicious white wine sauce and served with our magnificent home-made pasta. Or salad, if the lady is looking after her weight.' This, with a smirk towards Alice.

'No salad for me,' Alice said crisply. 'But the mussels sound lovely.'

'You don't want a starter?' Jeremy asked.

'No. But some bread would be nice.'

Jeremy ordered herb bread to begin with, and a bottle of white wine. A Chablis.

'A marvellous wine,' the redhead complimented. 'But then, you do know your wine, don't you, darling?'

She swanned off, leaving Alice exasperated and Jeremy blithely unconcerned.

'You've slept with her, haven't you?' Alice said.

Jeremy seemed startled by her accusatory tone.

'Only the once.'

Alice rolled her eyes at him in total exasperation.

'She was very upset one night,' he elaborated. 'It was a couple of years ago now. Her husband had just left her for another woman.'

'So you stayed and comforted her,' Alice said drily.

Jeremy smiled. 'I like you jealous.'

Alice pressed her lips tightly together lest she said something very unwise.

'No need to be jealous,' he went on. 'I don't really fancy Sophia, you see. I was just being kind.'

Alice had to laugh. She was still laughing when Sophia returned with a plate of bread. This time, she threw Alice a warm smile.

'That's better,' the older woman said. 'For a minute there I thought Jeremy had lost his mind, going out with someone so serious. He likes to have fun, my Jeremy, don't you, darling?' And she bent to give him a hug around his shoulders.

'I'm teaching Alice to have fun,' he said with a mischievous smile her way.

Alice stiffened when it looked as if Sophia was going to hug her as well. But she just leant close and whispered, 'Lucky girl,' in her ear before straightening and hurrying off again.

'What did she say to you?' Jeremy asked.

Alice gave him one of her cool looks. 'That's private.'

'I hope she didn't say anything uncomplimentary.'

'Not at all.'

'Good.'

A rather elderly Italian waiter brought the wine and a portable ice bucket, explaining as he opened it up then poured a taste-testing amount into Jeremy's glass that Sophia was busy with another customer and he'd be looking after their table for the rest of the evening. Alice hated feeling relieved at this news. Hated her jealousy as well. She didn't want to become emotionally involved with Jeremy. She just wanted to sleep with him. Which brought her to another matter that had begun bothering her.

'I don't think I can go to New York with you,' she said after the waiter had left and she'd indulged in a relaxing gulp of what was a truly delicious wine. A one-night stand with Jeremy was one thing. She could survive that. To spend a glamorous weekend with him in New York would be to risk becoming emotionally involved. She was already more emotionally involved with him than was wise.

Jeremy's blue eyes narrowed over the rim of his glass. 'Why not?'

'I can't really take the time off work.'

'That's just an excuse, Alice. Come on, don't start back-pedalling again.'

'Back-pedalling? What do you mean?'

'You know what I mean. That brute you dated has made you afraid of men. And nervous. You've no need to be nervous with me, Alice. Now no more nonsense, you're coming with me and that's that. I've already booked our hotel. It's a great hotel, and reasonably close to the theatre.'

'That was quick.'

'Had to be. With the premiere on that weekend all the hotels near the theatre involved have been heavily booked. To be honest, I couldn't get a normal room or even a normal suite, so I booked the honeymoon suite. Some lucky bastard had just cancelled.'

Alice bit her lip in an effort not to laugh. He really was a terrible cynic where marriage was concerned. But perversely funny at the same time.

'That was extravagant of you. And yes, before you say it, I know you can afford it.'

'I can. And speaking of money, once Alex sends his donation—Sergio's already sent his—you could well have enough to buy that house yourself, with some left over. That way, you won't have to feel beholden to me.'

'How did you know I didn't want that?'

'Alice, for pity's sake, it's obvious.'

Their meal arrived at that point, and Alice was left to mull over Jeremy's comment. She supposed she did have a heightened sense of independence, having vowed as a young girl never to rely on a man for anything. But she had good reasons for that, the same way Jeremy had good reasons for being anti-marriage.

'Time to eat, Alice,' he said. 'No more of that thinking.'

She glanced over at him and smiled. 'You're right.'

The food was delicious, the wine superb and the company highly entertaining. Alice almost forgot what was going to happen after they left the restaurant. But not quite. Jeremy insisted on dessert, claiming he had a sweet tooth. She wasn't sure exactly what he ordered, but when it came it looked decadent and very fattening, a large pastry case full of chocolate and custard, with more chocolate on the side. It proved to be as delicious as it looked. When the waiter asked if they wanted to order coffee, Jeremy glanced at her for her wishes and she shook her head, knowing that she couldn't sit there much longer thinking about *afterwards* back at his place. When he asked for the bill, she excused herself and dashed for the nearby powder room, not sure if her shaky legs and suddenly spinning head were due to the amount of wine she'd drunk or the imminence of what she was about to do. She was amazed that the small mirror above the wash basin didn't betray her inner feelings. Her bladder could certainly have just given testimony to her tension. But her face looked quite calm. Maybe she'd practised composure for so long that it was automatic. Still, it was better than looking as if she was about to fall apart with nerves.

When she presented herself back at the table, Jeremy was standing, waiting for her.

'Ready to go?' he asked her.

She was never going to be ready, Alice accepted. If she could have run away right now, she would have. But to do so would have been the ultimate in cowardice. Instead, she tightened her fluttering stomach and steeled her spine.

'Yes,' she said coolly.

CHAPTER FOURTEEN

JEREMY CONTAINED HIS frustration with difficulty as he escorted her from the restaurant. A few short minutes she'd been in that powder room, but in that brief time the warm, witty companion he'd been enjoying dinner with had disappeared, and in her place was the Ice Princess.

At least she was true to form, but did she have to revert to type just before he was about to enjoy what he'd been hoping to enjoy with her all damned week? Jeremy sympathised with what had happened to her but he refused to let her use it as an excuse not to live life to the full. Which was what he believed in. Living life to the full, which included a normal sex life.

'Are you all right to drive?' she asked pointedly once they were both back in his car.

'Perfectly,' he replied, turning on the engine and backing slowly out of his parking bay. 'I only had two glasses. You drank the rest.'

'Yes, I suppose I did. I was trying to relax, if you recall.'

'Something tells me you could do with another glass or two when you get to my place,' he said as he headed for home. 'You've gone all buttoned up on me again.'

Her sigh was long, and heavy. 'Sorry. Bit nervous.'

His irritation melted at her admission. 'I can understand that,' he said gently. 'It's your first time since that creep assaulted you. I promise not to rush things, Alice. And you can always say no at any stage. I'll stop straight away.'

The smile she slanted his way was heartbreakingly sweet. 'I can't imagine many girls saying no to you at any stage.'

'You have. Repeatedly.'

'True. Thank you for that reassurance, Jeremy. I needed to hear that.'

'My pleasure.'

After a few moments of a rather awkward silence, she said, 'You never did tell me how you came to be a billionaire.'

'You didn't ask.'

'I forgot. But I'm asking now.'

He gave her a potted history of how Sergio and Alex had found a rundown wine bar for sale near the university, which they'd thought had potential, and how he'd bankrolled them, via an inheritance he'd received from his grandmother. Then he went on to explain how they'd gradually acquired more wine bars all over England till it had become too much for them to manage, so they'd formed the WOW franchise. He was amazed that Alice hadn't heard of them—clearly she wasn't into wine bars—and had to explain that WOW meant Wild Over Wine. Finally, he told her that they'd sold the franchise last year to an American firm for a few billion.

'You must have been over the moon,' she said.

'I was. In a way. But not in another. Selling the franchise also meant a severing of our business relationship, so we don't see much of each other any more. Sergio went back to work in his family business in Milan and Alex returned to Australia to concentrate on property development back there. I miss them terribly. I can't wait to go to New York and see Sergio again. You'll like him, Alice. He's a great guy.'

'He must be if Bella married him. She wasn't exactly known for commitment, was she?'

'You can say that again. Hopefully, their marriage will work but who knows? I haven't much faith in marriage.'

'I'm a little of the same mind.'

This surprised him. Most girls he knew had romantic ideas about marriage.

'You don't want to get married?' he asked.

'Never in a million years.'

Jeremy should have been super pleased with this news. So why wasn't he?

Not that he was *dis*pleased. At least now he wouldn't have to worry about Alice wanting more from him than he could give.

'You're a most unusual girl,' he remarked. 'But who am I to judge? I believe marriage is the kiss of death when it comes to relationships.'

'Well, you don't have to worry about that,' she said with laughter in her voice. 'You don't *have* relationships. Women, for you, are just ships passing in the night.'

'Oh, come now. That's a bit harsh. I'll have you know that one of my girlfriends lasted for several weeks.'

'Really? What happened? Were you laid up with a broken leg or something?'

He laughed. 'Actually, I was. Skiing accident.'

Now she laughed. 'Thought as much.'

'Feeling a bit more relaxed now?' he asked hopefully as he turned down the cobbled street that led to his mews house.

'Much. Is this where you live?' she asked when he pulled up in front of his garage, lights automatically coming on when he pressed the remote for the door to roll up.

'Yes. This is home.'

'It's lovely.'

It *was* lovely. Two-storeyed, but with three entrances. One at the top of the ivy-clad iron-railed steps that led up to the first floor. One near the garage door on the bottom floor, and an internal door that led from the garage into the ground floor hallway. Not a large house by any means, but it suited Jeremy's bachelor lifestyle perfectly. He led her out of the garage and up the steps to the top floor, unlocking the heavy wooden door that led into the upstairs hallway, steering her into the main living room, which served as both lounge and dining areas. Depositing her on one of the large cream leather sofas that faced each other in front of the stone fireplace, he immediately went over to the drinks cabinet where he asked her what she wanted whilst he poured himself a rather stiff Scotch.

Alice was beyond wanting anything, except for him to start making love to her. But she smiled and said that perhaps she should stick to white wine. She knew from experience that mixing drinks did not sit well with her.

He nodded. 'There's a bottle of dry white in the fridge. I'll just get you a glass.'

When he disappeared through a doorway to his right, she allowed herself a deep sigh, then a long look around. The inside of his place was pretty much what she'd expected. Not quite a bachelor pad, but slick and modern, all polished wooden floors and leather furniture, with just enough wooden furniture to stop it from becoming too cold. All the tables were wood. And the lighting was nicely subtle, a small chandelier hanging over the dining table and standing lamps in the corners. She personally hated recessed lighting, though of course it was practical when you had low ceilings. Jeremy's ceilings weren't low, they were very high, telling of the Edwardian era in which this place had been originally built.

Jeremy returned with her glass of wine. Alice was proud of her hand for not shaking when she took it from him. He sat down close to her, having added ice to his own drink. They both sipped for a few seconds, then looked at each other and smiled, she nervously and he confidently. Jeremy soon took her glass and placed it along with his drink on the low coffee table before slowly, oh, so slowly, taking her into his arms. He didn't kiss her straight away, just looked deep into her eyes.

'Did I tell you tonight how beautiful I think you are?' he murmured.

* * *

Jeremy's phone ringing at that precise moment brought an uncharacteristic swear word to his lips. 'I meant to turn that damned thing off. It's Alex. The timing of that man! Do you mind, Alice? I won't be long.'

'Go ahead,' she told him.

He reached to give her back her glass of wine and put the phone to his ear.

'What's up, bro?'

'I've just become a father, mate. Would you believe that? *Me*. A father!'

'That's wonderful, Alex. Congratulations. How's Harriet?'

'Marvellous. God, but women are brave.'

'And the baby. How is he?'

'A right little corker. Big, like me. And smart as a whip. Do you know, he smiled at me within a minute of being born?'

'I think that might be gas, Alex.'

'Rubbish. Jeremy's going to be a genius.'

Jeremy's heart caught. 'You named him after me...'

'Too right. I always liked your name. It has class. His full name is Jeremy Sergio Kotana. Sounds good, doesn't it? And I promise I won't call him Jerry. Look, I can't stay and chat. I have to ring Sergio and then I'm going to help the nurse give my son his first bath. I'll send pictures.'

He hung up before Jeremy could say another word.

'That was Alex,' he said on picking up his own drink again. 'His wife's just had their baby. A boy. They named him Jeremy.'

Alice could see how touched Jeremy was, which touched her.

'He already thinks the boy's a genius. Ah, the optimism of new parents. But enough of that. Now where were we?'

'Have you turned your phone off?' Alice asked as he swooped on her drink again.

'Hell no. I'll do it as soon as I get rid of these glasses.'

Once empty-handed, he switched off his phone then returned to take her into his arms again, not quite so slowly this time. His head descended in a rush for which she was grateful. She didn't want any more time to think, or to worry.

His mouth was still gentle at first, his kiss seductive in its subtle demands. His nipping softly at her bottom lip eventually brought a low moan to her throat, her lips falling apart in open invitation. His tongue slid inside, entwining with hers in a highly erotic fashion before withdrawing. Her own tongue blindly followed his, seeking more. His lips clamped around the tip, sucking it ravenously. Again she moaned, twisting in his arms till somehow they were lying together on the sofa, face to face, mouths fused, their bodies jammed up against each other, his against the back of the sofa.

She felt his hand on her left leg. She wasn't wearing stockings, having shaved and moisturised her legs in anticipation of just such a moment. Her breath caught underneath his kiss as his hand travelled up under her skirt, getting closer and closer to where she was already burning for him. When it stopped mid-thigh, she almost cried out. Instead, she just kissed him harder. She even sucked on *his* tongue.

His hand moved again, but not to touch her more intimately. He caressed her thigh for a while before lifting his hand away. She wasn't aware of his undoing the buttons on her dress till her skirt fell open and she felt his hand on her belt. Wrenching her mouth away in surprise, she stared up into his face. But he wasn't looking at her. He was looking at what he was doing. The belt was quickly dispatched, and the remaining buttons flicked open. When he pushed her dress back off her shoulders, she lifted her body to help

him. He tossed her dress across the coffee table, then returned his attention to her body.

Her white satin bra surrendered to his fingers in no time,
leaving her with nothing on but her matching bikini briefs
and her nude sandals. When he laid her back on the sofa,
she went, her eyes dazed upon him. When he stood up,
she thought he was about to undress. But he didn't. He just
shrugged out of his suit jacket and took off his tie, throwing them next to her other clothes, startling her when he
knelt down on the rug next to the sofa. As his head started
to descend towards her bared breasts with their eager rock-
like nipples, Alice squeezed her eyes tightly shut.

Oh, Lord, she thought shakily.

No man had ever *seen* her breasts naked before, let alone
done what he was doing. In her teenage fantasies she'd
imagined a man kissing her nipples, but hadn't anticipated
how it would actually feel. It felt incredible, her back arch-
ing as he tugged on one nipple with his teeth whilst he
kneaded her other breast. Not roughly. Gently. Playfully.
Yet they soon became oversensitive. When she moaned her
discomfort, he stopped, licking the burning nipples over
and over till she sighed with pleasure. At the same time
one of his hands drifted down over her stomach, which
immediately tightened. Alice held her breath when he finally pushed her legs apart, her left leg dropping off the
edge of the sofa, her right leg moving restlessly, till it was
bent at the knee, her shoe digging into the sofa. He took
them off, oh, so slowly, caressing each foot as he went, her
eyes finally flinging open when his fingers brushed over
her ticklish toes.

'Don't!' she cried. 'I can't stand being tickled there.'

He just smiled. 'My apologies. Still, perhaps it's time
to adjourn to the bedroom.'

She gasped when he scooped her up into his arms as if
she were a feather. But as he carried her from the room, a
memory hit of another time when a man had carried her

into his bedroom, carried her there and dumped her onto his bed. He hadn't bothered to undress her, just ripped off her knickers. Hadn't bothered to undress himself, just undid his zipper and fell on top of her.

Jeremy didn't dump her onto his bed. He laid her down quite gently. And he did undress, quickly stripping down to his underpants.

Alice tried to recapture her earlier desire as she looked at his beautiful male body. But it was no use. The moment had gone, spoiled by that brute back at college, spoiled by her own irrational reaction. For Jeremy was nothing like that other man. She hated herself for saying no at this last stage but it had to be done before he became embarrassingly naked.

'Jeremy,' she said sharply with a tidal wave of regret.

'What?' he asked, his expression freezing.

'I'm sorry,' she choked out. 'I… I can't.'

'Can't what?'

'I can't do this. I'm saying no.'

Disbelief ripped through Jeremy. Disbelief and frustration. Surely she couldn't expect him to stop at this late stage. Surely not!

But one look at her anguished eyes told him that she did. He couldn't help it. He swore.

'I'm so sorry,' she blurted out. 'I didn't mean for this to happen. I'm not a tease. Honestly. I… Oh, God…' With a sob, she covered her face with her hands, rolled over and burst into tears.

Jeremy's frustration disappeared in the face of her distress. And so did his erection. Sitting down on the bed behind her, he reached out to pat her shaking shoulder with a gentle hand. 'Please don't cry, Alice. It's all right. Truly, it is.'

'No, it's not,' she blubbered into her hands. 'I've ruined everything, me and my crazy screwed-up mind.'

Clearly, this all went back to that date rape. Or near date rape. Jeremy wondered just how far the creep had got before she was able to stop him. 'Is there anything I can say to help?'

She rolled back over, her face all red and tear-streaked. 'Like what? Look, don't waste any more time on me, Jeremy. It's useless. I'm useless. If I can't be a normal woman with someone like you then there's no hope for me.'

Jeremy heard a compliment in there somewhere.

Before he could think of what to say next she was up off the bed and striding from the room, her shoulders squared in an attitude of fierce determination.

'Would you please call me a taxi?' she threw over her shoulder as she made her way across the hall and back into the living room. By the time he dragged on his trousers and caught up with her, she was already dressing.

'There's no need for a taxi,' he said. 'I'll drive you home.'

'Absolutely not! You just had a whisky. You'll be over the limit.'

'I didn't drink all of it.'

'You drank enough. For pity's sake, Jeremy, stop playing the gentleman,' she snapped, doing up her last button with angry fingers. 'And just call me a taxi.'

He called her a taxi.

'I'll ring you tomorrow,' he said whilst they waited for the taxi to arrive.

'Please don't.' Her voice was as cold as her face.

'Why not?'

The look she gave him said it all. 'Because I don't want you to. Move on to someone else. Someone who'll give you what you want, because it's painfully obvious that I can't.'

'What if I said I don't want anyone else? I just want you.'

'You don't. Not really. I was just the girl who dared to say no. I was a challenge, Jeremy, one which you went to great lengths to meet. Which reminds me. Please don't feel obliged to continue pretending interest in my charity. You and I both know that was just a ploy to see me again. Underneath, I knew that all along.'

He didn't deny it. How could he? It was true. But only in the beginning. Still, she wouldn't believe him if he told her that he'd come to truly care about what she was doing for those poor women. That it had made him feel good, helping them. He couldn't win, no matter what he said.

He had to let her go. For now, that was. But he had no intention of giving up on her.

He wanted her. And she wanted him. He just had to find a way past the mental blockage that was haunting her. She couldn't go her whole life being afraid of men, and sex. It wasn't healthy.

'What about the house I was going to help you buy?'

'Forget that. If you're right about your rich friends coming through with their donations then the charity will be able to afford to buy the house.'

'I'm still going to call you.'

She sighed and picked up her bag. 'Do what you like. You will, anyway. But I won't be going out with you again, Jeremy. Trust me on that.'

'We'll see,' he bit out.

'No. *You'll* see.'

A horn honking outside signalled that the taxi had arrived. Suddenly her eyes softened on him, her face full of regret.

'I'm not angry with you. Truly. I'm angry with myself. You have been a gentleman through and through, for which I am profoundly grateful. Goodbye, Jeremy.' At the last moment she came forward and kissed him gently on the cheek. And then she was gone, bolting out of the room, and his home.

Jeremy stood there, frozen to the spot, as he listened to the banging of a car door and the sound of the taxi moving off. Finally his hand lifted to touch the moist spot where her lips had met his skin.

'It's not over, Alice,' he muttered as his chest squeezed tight. 'Not by a long shot.'

CHAPTER FIFTEEN

'COME IN, MADGE,' Jeremy said when his PA knocked. It was just before five the following Friday afternoon, Jeremy's mood not matching his new sales figures, which were great. Ken's e-Books were going from strength to strength.

Madge came in, looking very well groomed, he finally noticed, and wearing a dress he hadn't seen before. Jeremy wondered if dear old Kenneth had something to do with that as well.

'I just had a rather surprising call from Alice,' she said straight away.

'Surprising in what way?' he replied, taken aback that she'd called his office at all.

'She thanked me for the work I'd done setting up the website, then said she would take it from there. When I asked if she wanted to speak to you, she said "no, thank you very much." Then hung up.'

'I see,' he said, sighing. He'd refrained from ringing her all week, hoping that time would be on his side. Clearly, not.

'Things didn't work out between you and Alice last weekend, then?' Madge asked gently.

'How did…?' Jeremy stopped, remembering their behaviour in that wine bar last Friday night. Anyone would have seen how taken they were with each other. But it hadn't been enough to overcome her fears.

'No,' he said simply. 'Things didn't work out.' Finally, he was beginning to accept that it was over before it had even begun. Never before had he felt so down. Or so alone.

'What a shame. I thought she was perfect for you.'

Jeremy shook his head at Madge, not sure how she came to that conclusion. So he asked.

Madge shrugged. 'Hard to put my finger on it. She just was.'

'Thank you for your insight, Madge,' he said drily. But he knew what she was getting at. Alice's appeal was as mysterious as she was.

'Why don't you try again?' she asked. 'You know the old adage. If at first you don't succeed…'

'Maybe I will,' he said, not very convincingly.

'Maybes won't cut the mustard, boss. Where there's a will there's a way.'

Jeremy had to laugh. 'Enough of the sayings, Madge. All right. I'll ring her. Tonight.'

'Good idea. By the way, thought you might like to know that Ken and I have become an item.'

'I thought there had to be a reason behind the new dress. Going anywhere special tonight?'

'To a concert. A rock concert. Ken said we had to widen our horizons further. Then tomorrow we're going up in a hot-air balloon.'

'Good for you. Have fun, then.'

'I will.'

She sashayed out, humming happily to herself. Amazing what a fun relationship could do for one's attitude to life. He'd wanted to show Alice how to have fun. But he doubted that would happen now. Still, he did have to try again, or he'd never be able to live with himself. Yet by a quarter to eight that night, he still hadn't rung Alice. No man liked constant rejection, and Jeremy wasn't different from any other man.

'Ring the girl, you coward,' he lectured himself after the clock ticked over to eight.

Snatching up his phone from where it was sitting on a side table, he brought up her number and pressed.

'Alice Waterhouse,' she answered on the third ring.

'Alice. It's Jeremy. Please don't hang up,' he added, his heart racing in his chest.

Her sigh wafted down the line. 'All right,' she said. 'What do you want?'

'Just to talk to you. Maybe take you for coffee somewhere. Are you home or at work?'

'I'm still at work. One of the case workers went home sick so I have to stay late.'

'How late?'

'Not sure. Ten. Maybe eleven.'

'You will take a taxi home, won't you? Not the Tube.'

'I will take whatever I want to take, Jeremy,' she said coolly.

The thought of her walking to the station, alone, at that time on a Friday night worried him sick.

'Call me when you're finished and I'll come and drive you home.'

She didn't answer him for a few seconds. 'That won't be necessary. I'll take a taxi.'

He didn't believe her. 'Promise?'

'Jeremy, might I remind you that you are not my boyfriend.'

'I know that. But I am your friend. And I miss you.'

He heard her sharply sucked-in breath.

'Will you go somewhere for coffee with me tomorrow?' he asked. 'Just coffee.'

There was resignation in her sigh. 'Why won't you give up?'

'I like you too much for that, Alice.'

Another heart-stopping silence.

'Ring me tomorrow,' she said at long last. 'Now I really must go. A new client has just arrived.'

Alice had lied. There was no new client. They were having another blessedly quiet Friday night. But she simply hadn't been able to talk to Jeremy any longer. This last week had seen her besieged with regret and remorse. She really had treated him very poorly. He'd been so nice to her. He was still being nice.

She'd missed him too. Way too much. He filled her mind every moment of every day. She'd found it difficult to concentrate on her counselling all week. She despised herself for not being able to go through with things last Saturday night. She was sure it would have been a memorable experience, if only she could have overcome her silly fears. His lovemaking on that sofa had been amazing. He'd be a fantastic lover. Unfortunately, she couldn't say the same for herself. She would never be a fantastic lover. She'd always be waiting for one of those hideous memories to hit, dampening her desire as if she'd had a bucket of iced water thrown over her. Far better that she continue with her dateless, celibate lifestyle. It wasn't as though she wanted to get married. She did crave being normal, however. And she craved Jeremy. Crazy, really.

She should never have agreed to have coffee with him. Well, she hadn't really agreed yet. When he rang her tomorrow she could say no again. The trouble was that saying no to Jeremy was always very, very hard...

By ten o'clock, Alice started to yawn. It had been a long day. And a long week. Finally, she stood up from behind her desk and went to find Jane, telling her that she was going home. She momentarily considered calling a taxi but she didn't have all that much money with her. Saving for her flat had now become more important to her than ever before. Slipping on her black jacket, she looped her carryall over her left shoulder and headed for the door.

It was cold outside, and pitch-black, clouds blanketing the sky. The street lights weren't all that great, either. And did not work very often. Feeling unusually nervous—Jeremy had put bad thoughts into her mind—Alice put her head down and started to hurry along the street. She'd only gone a couple of blocks when two young men in hoodies stepped out in front of her from a darkened alley, forcing her to stop. They were probably just teenagers, but well grown, and tough-looking.

'Goin' somewhere in a hurry, love?' the taller one said, his voice slurred.

Whilst fear had Alice's heart slamming against her ribs, she tried not to look scared to death.

'Get out of my way,' she snapped, reaching for the rape alarm that she always kept in her bag. 'Or I'll call the police.'

'Not wiffou' your phone, darlin',' the other boy said, wrenching the bag off her shoulder.

A scream came to Alice's throat but never made it past her lips. The first man was behind her in an instant, one arm snaked around her waist, the other clamped over her mouth.

'Be nice to me, sweetheart,' he whispered in her ear as he pushed her towards the alley, 'and you won't get hurt. All we want is what yuh give the boyfriend every night. He won't miss it. Honest.'

Alice was already crying inside when, suddenly, she was free, a familiar voice echoing in the night air. 'Are you all right, Alice?' Jeremy asked.

A shaking Alice stared up at him. 'I… I think so…'

'Well, well, if it isn't the boyfriend,' the leader said smarmily, despite having been yanked aside with relative ease. 'A fancy man to go with little Miss Fancy Pants. You fink you can take the two of us, matey?'

Alice couldn't believe the smile of satisfaction that crossed Jeremy's handsome face. 'Won't be a sec, Alice.'

She watched, stunned, whilst Jeremy had both of her assailants flat on their backs in no time, using his feet and his hands in a display of martial arts that was as unexpected as it was impressive. They weren't unconscious but they were moaning and groaning, one clutching his groin whilst the other writhed on the ground in pain.

Jeremy returned to put a comforting arm around her

still-trembling body as he whipped out his phone and rang the police.

She only half listened as he relayed what had happened and where they were, her mind distracted with horrible thoughts. What if Jeremy hadn't rescued her? What if...?

'Let's go, Alice,' Jeremy said, taking her arm and steering her across the street to where his car was parked by the kerb.

'But shouldn't we wait for the police?' she asked, still shaking with shock.

'We are. I just think you need to sit down. You're in shock.'

'Oh.'

He'd just seen her safely seated in the passenger seat when the police arrived.

'Stay right where you are, Alice,' Jeremy told her. 'I'll handle this.'

The police locked the still-stunned offenders in the back of their van before talking to Jeremy for a few minutes, taking notes. Meanwhile the female police officer came over to talk to Alice, gently leading her through what had happened before getting her to sign a witness statement. In less than ten minutes the police were gone.

Alice's head was still reeling when Jeremy got back into the car, carrying her dropped handbag with him.

'You okay?' he asked with a worried look her way.

'I will be,' she reassured him.

'You'll be pleased to know that the police recognised those two. They're on parole for various offences so they'll be going straight back to jail.'

Alice sighed a shaky sigh. 'That's a relief. I wasn't looking forward to having to give evidence in court. Though I would have, if I had to. I can't stop thinking what might have happened if you hadn't come along.'

'No point in thinking like that, Alice,' he said sternly.

'I did come along and nothing happened. Now let's get you home.'

As he drove off, Alice stared over at him, still amazed at the ease with which he'd dispensed with those two thugs. 'You've done that kind of thing before, haven't you?'

'Only once,' he said. 'In my second last year at school. A young boy was being bullied, the way I'd been bullied. Till I grew tall and took up Kung Fu, karate and kick-boxing, that is. When I came across a couple of big boys humiliating this poor defenceless little kid, old tapes went off and I decided to put all those martial arts lessons I'd taken to good use.' A self-satisfied smile pulled at Jeremy's mouth. 'Trust me when I say those two never bullied another boy. Not whilst I was there, anyway.'

'You became a hero,' she said, awe in her voice.

His smile turned wry. 'Not according to the headmaster. I was almost expelled.'

'Well, I think you're a hero. You were my hero tonight.'

'Glad to be of service.'

'Of course, I'm not sure what you were doing there in the first place. You weren't stalking me, were you?'

'Absolutely not. I simply didn't trust you not to take the Tube, so I was on my way to drive you home when I passed you in the street. You'd left earlier than you said, you naughty girl.'

'I should have called a taxi, like *you* said.'

'Yes, you should have.'

'I will, in the future.' Lord, yes. No way would she risk having what happened tonight happening ever again. Another deep shudder ran through her. What if Jeremy *hadn't* saved her...?

'You're still in shock,' Jeremy pronounced. 'You need someone to be with you tonight, Alice. Is your flatmate home? Can I safely leave you in her hands to look after you, or do you want me to stay with you?'

As Jeremy pulled up outside her flat, Alice decided that

another white lie was called for. She needed to be alone to de-stress, and to think, *without* Jeremy's disturbing presence.

'Yes, Fiona's home. See?' she said, pointing to the light in the front room. That's her bedroom.' It was a habit they'd got into when they went out, to fool the baddies. How naive could they be?

'At least let me walk you to the door,' Jeremy insisted.

When they got there, he drew her into his arms and hugged her tightly.

'God, Alice. I nearly died when I saw that man with his filthy hands on you.'

Alice's heart turned over at the depth of emotion in Jeremy's voice. He cared about her. He really did.

'My hero,' she murmured, and hugged him back.

'I wouldn't go that far.'

'I would.'

'Look, I don't like leaving you.'

'I'll be all right. Truly,' she reassured him.

'I'll be ringing you tomorrow.'

She nodded. 'I'd like that. But not too early.'

'You won't change your mind in the morning?'

'No,' she said, a plan already forming in her surprisingly clear mind. 'I won't.'

CHAPTER SIXTEEN

JEREMY WOKE AROUND NINE, astonished at how good a night's sleep he'd had. Possibly because Alice had agreed to at least talk to him. He hoped she'd slept okay, hoped that flatmate of hers had given her the comfort and support she'd obviously needed. Being grabbed like that after her other earlier assault must have been terrifying. It didn't bear thinking about what they would have done to Alice, if he hadn't come along. He needed to get through to her today to never take such a risk again.

Though perhaps she already knew that. Alice was a sensible young woman. She was also, however, incredibly stubborn.

Rising, Jeremy showered and shaved before pulling on some casual clothes. Dark blue jeans. A pale blue polo. No shoes. He padded, barefooted, into the kitchen where he poured himself some muesli and orange juice. After breakfast, he went down to his den where he spent some time answering emails on his computer—Alex had sent more photos of his baby boy and Sergio wanted details of his booking arrangements for the weekend in New York. He told Sergio he was definitely bringing someone with him, hoping against hope that Alice would agree to come. But he wasn't supremely confident. He was never supremely confident where Alice was concerned. Damn, but he hated that.

By noon, Jeremy was itching to call her. He was about to reach for his phone when it rang. When the screen showed it was Alice calling, his stomach tightened with a sudden jab of fear. As he put the phone to his ear, he told himself not to be such a fool. She wouldn't be mean to him after last night. Surely not.

'Hello, Alice?' he answered. 'I was just about to call you.'

'That's nice,' she said coolly. Too coolly for his liking. 'I was wondering,' she added, 'if you would like to come over to my place tonight and I'll cook you dinner. As a way of thanking you for what you did last night. But also to talk. Fiona's gone to Paris with her fiancé for the weekend so we'll be alone.'

For a split second Jeremy didn't know what to think. Was she suggesting what he thought she was suggesting? Why mention that her flatmate had gone away if she didn't want him to stay the night? Surely she would know exactly what her invitation was implying.

How brave she was to try again so soon, he thought. How wonderfully, incredibly brave. That was why she was trying to sound so cool. He'd figured out a while back that her Ice Princess act was just a façade. Underneath, she was all warm woman. With hang-ups, admittedly. And quite a lot of emotional baggage. But he knew what to expect now. He could work out in advance what to do, and what not to do.

'I'd like that,' he said. Which was the understatement of the year. He'd wanted to make love to Alice from the first moment he'd seen her, his desire for her the strongest he'd ever experienced. He'd been suppressing that desire this past week, because he'd thought it was futile. But it had always been there, flickering away like a fire down to its last ashes. It had only taken one small gust of hope to make the dying flames flare up again into a fire that would burn bright all day.

'What time would you like me to be there?' he said, thinking he'd race over there now if she'd like.

'Would seven o'clock be too early?'

'Not at all. Should I bring wine?'

'Absolutely not. No wine. I will provide the wine. And no flowers. Or chocolates. This is my treat.'

'You should never tell a man not to bring chocolates and flowers.'

'Perhaps, but that's what I want. Just bring yourself.'

'Just myself,' he echoed. And lots of condoms...

The thought set his desire into overdrive. Lord, but he'd have to do something to dampen *that* down before tonight. He couldn't imagine anything worse than showing up at Alice's place with an obvious hard-on. As much as she might want him to stay the night, he would have to be careful not to frighten her, or to rush anything.

'Casual dress?' he asked her.

'That would be perfect.'

'I'll look forward to it. Now before you go, did you sleep okay? Did Fiona take care of you last night?'

Another of her telling silences.

Jeremy sighed. 'She wasn't there, was she? You were all alone.'

'Yes, I was alone, but I was fine,' she said crisply. 'It saved me having to explain what happened. There's no point in going on and on about it, is there? A miss is as good as a mile.'

'True.' Jeremy empathised with Alice's pragmatism, but he wasn't convinced she wasn't still somewhat traumatised by last night's events. He decided then and there to talk to her at length tonight before attempting any lovemaking. It would kill him, but it was the right thing to do.

'I should go, Jeremy, I have lots to do to get ready for tonight.'

'Shall I hope for *cordon bleu* cooking?'

She laughed. It was a lovely sound. 'You can hope but you won't get. I'm a competent enough cook, but not a chef.'

'I will still look forward to it.'

Which was his second understatement of the year.

'That's good,' she said cheerily, and hung up, leaving Jeremy fizzing with a frustrating mixture of excitement and anticipation. How he was going to get through this day was anyone's guess!

Seven saw him outside Alice's place, having walked there, not wanting to have to watch what he drank. He suspected he might need a glass or three to settle his own nerves. Amazing for him to feel nervous over making love to a woman but there it was. In two short weeks Alice had managed to totally turn him inside out. He'd even dithered over what to wear, finally settling on beige trousers and a mustard-yellow polo that he hadn't worn in ages, but which Sergio had once said suited him. With the evening promising to be cool with the forecast of drizzle, he'd thrown on a brown suede jacket, which had cost him a mint at an exclusive menswear store in Milan and which he'd rarely worn. If truth be told, he had way too many clothes, a symptom he'd read somewhere of loneliness. At the time he'd dismissed such a notion as laughable. Now he wasn't so sure.

Jeremy took a deep breath then rang the bell.

After a short delay, Alice opened the door looking delicious in white trousers and that pretty floral blouse she'd been wearing last week. Her fair hair was down, curling softly around her shoulders. Her make-up was minimal, her lipstick a delicate coral colour. Her feet were shod in flat white sandals, her toenails painted a bright red. Not her fingernails, however, which were unpainted but shiny.

'Where's your car?' were her first words.

Dismay sent Jeremy's stomach plummeting, but he didn't let it show. He supposed it had been optimistic of him to think Alice would want him to make love to her after what had happened to her last night. Clearly, this dinner invite was a gesture of gratitude, not a desire to try again.

He hoped his shrug looked suitably nonchalant. 'It's a nice night. I thought I'd walk.'

'But it's supposed to rain later.'

'Is it? I'm sure I can borrow an umbrella, if need be.'

She gave him a frowning look. 'I suppose so. Come in.

Let me take your jacket. It's quite warm inside. I've had the oven on for hours.'

She hung his jacket on a coat stand near the door, then led him down the hallway into a kitchen that wasn't overly large but which had been renovated at some stage to make use of every inch. The cupboards were white, the counter tops and small breakfast bar made of black granite, and the two stools white with stainless-steel bases. All the appliances were stainless steel, including the oven from which wafted the mouth-watering aroma of roast lamb.

'Smells good,' he said, sliding up onto one of the stools whilst she picked up an oven mitt and had a quick peek.

'Bronwyn once told me that men liked roast dinners more than anything, so I decided to give it a whirl. To be honest, this is my first roast dinner and I'm beginning to wish I'd made stir-fry.'

'I'm sure it'll be great. And who's Bronwyn?'

'She was the cook at home when I was growing up.'

'And home is…where?' he prompted. Though of course he already knew.

'In Dorset,' was her curt reply.

'No kidding. My family home is in Cornwall. We could almost be neighbours.'

'Not quite. There's a whole county between us. Would you mind opening the wine?' she asked, putting two bottles of red onto the breakfast bar along with a bottle opener. 'It's not the kind that unscrews. I meant to open a bottle earlier and let it breathe but I've been flat out with setting the table and the dinner as well as trying to look presentable.'

'You look lovely,' he said as he picked up the first bottle and glanced at the label. 'Good Lord, Alice, this is very expensive wine. It must have cost you heaps, especially if you bought it at the local bottle shop.'

'I didn't have to buy it,' she confessed. 'Fiona had a birthday party a little while back and these were left over. Some rich friend of her father's sent over a case. Red wine isn't to Fiona's personal taste and she said I could have it, if and when I needed a drink. I don't think she knew how good a wine it is.'

'But *you* knew.'

'Oh, yes. My father gave me a first-class education in wine, especially red wine. He had a marvellous cellar, full of the best wines from all over the world. Or he did, till he got into debt and had to sell everything off. It upset him so much that he went down in the empty cellar one day and shot himself.'

'Good grief,' Jeremy said, amazed at how calmly she'd relayed this news; amazed too that she was telling him such a personal detail. Why? he wondered.

'It was a terrible shock at first,' she went on, getting two wineglasses down from a cupboard and placing them on the breakfast bar. 'I was only ten. But not as big a shock as when my older sister, Marigold, married one short year later, her husband proving to be one of those abusive partners whose wives I try to counsel.'

Jeremy didn't know what to say, so he didn't. He just opened the wine and poured. Alice picked up one of the glasses and drank a decent mouthful.

'When I told my mother that Rupert was hitting Marigold behind closed doors, she refused to believe me. When I made a right old fuss, she packed me off to boarding school. Which Rupert paid for, of course. He was very rich, you see, and had repaid all of Daddy's debts as well as bankrolled the lifestyle which Mother had grown used to.'

Jeremy was beginning to get a good picture of what had fashioned Alice's character. No wonder she didn't trust men. The surprise was that he was here at all! Once again, he wondered why. Something was going on here that he wasn't privy to. Yet.

'As you can imagine, I didn't cry when Rupert was killed in a motorcycle accident last year. Couldn't have happened to a nicer man,' she added, lifting her glass in a mock toast.

'Did they have children?' Jeremy asked.

Alice's face softened. 'Yes, a dear little boy. Dickie. He'll be four soon. His father doted on him, of course. It was just the mother he loathed. And loved, according to Marigold.' Alice shook her head in exasperation. 'She has no idea what true love is.'

'Do *you*, Alice?'

'I know what it isn't.'

'Why are you telling me all this?'

She looked at him long and hard. 'Because I want you to know why I am as I am. Because I'm going to give you a truly difficult job to do. Because I think you're the only man who could do it even remotely right.'

Jeremy didn't have a clue what she was getting at. 'Might I ask what this difficult job entails?'

She took another huge gulp of wine. 'I wasn't going to ask you at the beginning of the evening. I was going to feed you and get you a bit tipsy. And me a lot tipsy. And when I thought the time was right, after I'd explained everything I just explained, *then* I was going to ask you. But nerves are playing havoc with my plans and now I'm just going to say it.'

'Say what?' he demanded impatiently.

Her eyes were suddenly full of fear. But then she scooped in a deep breath, lifted her chin up and said, 'I want you to take my virginity.'

There! She'd said it!

He just stared at her, his beautiful blue eyes wide, his whole body stilled with shock. His wineglass was mid-air, his hand frozen.

After what seemed like an eternity he put down his glass and stood up.

'No, Alice,' he said, his voice even deeper than usual. 'No. I don't do love or marriage or broken hearts. So I definitely don't do virgins.'

'But I don't want your love!' she protested. 'And I certainly don't want marriage,' she insisted. 'So my heart won't be broken. All I want is your kindness. And your expertise.'

'My...expertise,' he repeated, clearly taken aback. Possibly even offended. Which was the last thing she wanted.

'Yes. I already know first-hand about your lovemaking skills. Before I went bonkers the other night, I was having a wonderful time. Honestly. You were great. I can't think of any man I've ever met who's made me want to have sex with him more than you.'

'Obviously,' he said in droll tones. 'Since you haven't had sex with any man at all!'

She tried not to blush but it was futile.

'Which brings us to the question of why that is, Alice. You're...how old?' he asked as he slowly sat back down.

'Twenty-five.'

'Twenty-five,' he echoed, amazement in his voice.

She supposed it *was* pretty amazing in this day and age.

Jeremy shook his head from side to side in an attitude of disbelief. 'I could understand you being turned off men and sex after your near date rape, but that didn't happen all that long ago, so...'

'Five years,' she broke in. 'It happened five years ago.'

'Still no excuse,' he refuted bluntly. 'What about before that, when you were working as a model? And what about during all your teenage years when your hormones were going wild? Or are you saying you didn't fancy anyone enough then as well? I mean, you did come home from school on holidays, didn't you? I know I did. I made good damn use of them with the opposite sex. I lost *my* virginity at fourteen.'

'Well, bully for you!' Alice snapped, frustration finally getting the better of her. 'But we're not all like you, Jeremy, where sex is just fun and games. Some of us—teenage females especially—like to think they're in love to have sex.

And that just wasn't going to happen to me after what I'd seen Marigold's husband do to her. So if you don't mind, try to have a little sensitivity where my lack of sexual experience is concerned.'

'You're not in love with *me*, are you?' he asked, looking horrified.

'Certainly not.'

'That's a relief.'

She threw him a caustic glare. 'I've finally grown up enough to know that one's libido is not necessarily connected with love. To use your own words, Jeremy, I fancy you.'

'That's good. I can handle being fancied. I can't handle being loved. That's a deal breaker for me, Alice. I'm not into love.'

'Tell me something I don't already know,' she bit out whilst her heart squeezed out a small warning.

'The dinner's in danger of burning,' he said with a wry smile.

'Oh, Lord!' she exclaimed, whirling to open the oven. 'Oh, thank heavens, it's not really burnt. Just a bit singed around the edges. But I hope you like crispy potatoes,' she added as she grabbed two oven mitts and lifted the baking dish out of the oven, placing it on the draining tray next to the sink.

'I *love* crispy potatoes,' he assured her.

'Well, at least he loves something,' she muttered under her breath.

'What was that?'

'Nothing. Why don't you go into the dining room and light the candles? There's a box of matches on the table. And take the wine and glasses with you. I shouldn't be too long. I've already made the gravy. You do like gravy, don't you?'

'I love gravy.'

Alice almost laughed.

* * *

Jeremy was touched by how much trouble she'd gone to with the table, the elegant setting reminding him that Alice was, after all, the daughter of an earl. She would have been brought up with fine things, and to do things the right way. But as he lit the candles his mind wasn't on her aristocratic heritage, but on the 'job' she wanted him to do for her.

Never in his wildest dreams had he imagined Alice was a virgin. She was far too beautiful and far too sexy, once she let her guard down. The way she'd kissed him had shown a highly passionate nature. It had just been her wretched background, and that other unfortunate happening, he decided, that had forced her into adopting a manner that kept men at bay. Fear—and a lack of trust—had been the overriding factors that resulted in her being a virgin at twenty-five. Now that he thought about it more deeply, Alice was right. It had been insensitive of him to act so shocked, and to question her like that.

Jeremy vowed to do better in the future. Refilling their glasses with wine, he sat down and started giving the situation some serious thought. Clearly, she'd been going to go to bed with him last Saturday night, but at the last second she'd gone into a meltdown. He recalled this had happened shortly after he'd carried her into the bedroom. He couldn't be sure but he suspected that other creep might have done something similar.

Right, Jeremy thought. No carrying. No playing macho man. Nothing like that. His approach would have to be very different.

When Alice came into the room with their meals, looking pleased with herself, the thought popped into Jeremy's head that Alice liked being in control. Which gave him an idea...

CHAPTER SEVENTEEN

'I MIGHT TRY another roast some day,' Alice said after they'd both polished off their meals in double-quick time. 'I was worried for a minute there that I'd spoiled everything.'

She placed her knife and turned-over fork down in the middle of the plate before glancing up at Jeremy, her nerves still strung tight. 'I haven't, have I, Jeremy? Spoiled everything?'

They hadn't talked much whilst they ate, their only conversation about the food and the wine, and the rain outside.

His warm smile set her heart fluttering.

'Not in the slightest,' he said. 'I was just startled there, for a minute or two.'

'You understand why I'm still a virgin, then? You don't mind any more?'

His smile turned rueful. 'Of course I mind. It goes against my principles to deflower virgins. But there are exceptions to every rule and you, sweet Alice, are undoubtedly the exception.'

'Oh…' He was just so nice. She knew she was right to do this. If only she could stop her hands from shaking. And her insides.

'I have been giving the matter some further thought, however,' he went on, his voice serious, 'and I have decided not to make love to you tonight.'

Her dismay was as great as her frustration.

'I want *you* to make love to *me*,' he added with a wickedly sexy sparkle in his eyes.

Was she shocked? Relieved? Or simply terrified?

'But I can't!' she blurted out. 'I mean… I wouldn't know what to do!'

'Come now, Alice, you're a well-educated girl,' he said as he sat back and took another sip of wine. 'You've read lots of books and seen lots of movies. On top of that, you have a highly passionate nature. You'll work it out.'

All the air left Alice's lungs in a rush. 'Oh, Lord...'

'No need for prayers. Just do what comes naturally.'

'But...but...'

He put his glass down and stood up, holding his hand out to her. She stood up somewhat shakily and put her hand in his.

'Before we do this, Alice,' he said, his beautiful blue eyes softly caressing, 'I want you to know how much I admire you. And desire you. I've wanted you since the first moment I set eyes on you.'

His romantic words thrilled her and soothed her at the same time. Never had her decision to go to bed with Jeremy seemed so right. She suddenly felt like the most desirable woman in the world. And totally, wonderfully safe.

His eyes suddenly changed from soft to very sexy. 'Now lead me to your bedroom, Alice, where I want you to have your wicked way with me. But be gentle. It's been a while...'

She couldn't help it. She laughed, and in doing so released the rest of her tension. At the same time, her excitement level soared. She could hardly wait to have her wicked way with him. And she did know what to do, really. She'd been doing it in her head from the first moment she'd set eyes on him...

When Alice led him across the hallway into her stylishly furnished bedroom with its thankfully queen-sized bed, Jeremy wished he weren't quite so aroused, worried that the extent and size of his erection might frighten her. Not that she seemed overly frightened. He'd been right to give her control of tonight. It was what she needed this first time. To be in control.

'Do you want me to undress you, mistress?' he asked on a teasing note once they were standing by her bed with its delicate floral duvet and mountain of decorative pillows. 'Or would you rather I undress first?'

Her eyes widened at this last suggestion.

'I am yours to command,' he added, and waited avidly for her reaction.

She stared at him for a long moment before sucking in a deep breath then letting it out slowly. Her chin lifted slightly. 'That sounds like an excellent idea,' she said coolly as she tossed some of the excess pillows onto an antique armchair in the corner of the room. 'Once you're naked I want you to lie down on top of the bed.'

Good God, he thought as his loins leapt. She didn't take much encouragement, did she?

She sat on the end of the bed whilst he undressed slowly, her eyes glued to him all the while. It was shockingly exciting. And something Jeremy had never done before. Her big blue eyes definitely rounded when he finally divested himself of his underpants and stood there in front of her in all his naked glory. He was dying for her to touch him, or to stand up and kiss him. But she did neither, and he didn't dare make a move towards her. Instead, he did as ordered and lay down on the bed, crossing his ankles as he linked his hands up behind his head in a casual, non-threatening attitude. He didn't say a word, just waited for her to make the next move.

Two emotions swept through Alice as she got to her feet. Disbelief that she was actually doing this. And that Jeremy seemed to like it. Though, of course, he'd suggested the idea in the first place. Amazing, that. But her overriding emotion was a desire so fierce and so strong that it was rattling her brains. What it was doing to her body was equally powerful. She could actually feel the heat between her thighs. Her heart was hammering away, her stomach as tight as a drum. And her nipples... Oh, God, she didn't want to know what they would look like once she took off her bra. Which was what she was about to do. Not just her bra but all of her clothes. Every last stitch.

Why weren't her hands shaking, she wondered, as she undid the buttons of her blouse?

Because they weren't. They were quite steady, focusing on what they were doing instead of what was going on in her head. After she'd taken off her blouse she took off her trousers, kicking off her sandals as she did so. Her eyes went to his when she bent her arms around to unhook her bra. He wasn't ogling her, but he was definitely watching closely. After a brief hesitation, she did the deed, exposing her hard-tipped breasts to his gaze, her own eyes looking down as she took off her knickers, afraid suddenly that he wouldn't like the way she'd shaven her whole pubic area that day. She'd read somewhere that some men liked that look, but maybe he didn't. She needn't have worried, his admiring expression told her when she finally looked up again.

'Beautiful Alice,' he complimented in that incredible voice of his. 'And so, so sexy.'

She did feel sexy. Extremely sexy.

Climbing onto the bed was not easy, her nerves returning as she stretched out on her side next to him. She tried not to look directly at his erection but it was difficult.

'You don't have much body hair,' she said as she ran her fingers through the small smattering of light brown curls in the centre of his chest.

'No. I did have my chest waxed once but it hurt like hell, so I let it grow again.'

'Should I kiss you first?' she asked, her confidence taking another dive.

'You should do whatever you want to do, Alice. I'm easy.'

But when she slid down his body and did what she

wanted to do—what she'd been thinking of doing all day—
his hips jerked up, his ankles unhooked and his arms shot
out from behind his head.

'Hell, Alice,' he protested when she stared up at him,
her face all flushed and hot.

'Was I doing it wrong?' she asked breathlessly.

'Hardly. I just wasn't ready for that. I mean… I'm just a
tad excited, woman, in case you hadn't noticed. I've been
trying to relax, but that striptease of yours undid me entirely.'

Alice liked the sound of that. She smiled a rather naughty
smile.

'I didn't realise you were so…'

'So what?' he growled.

'So into me,' she said cheekily.

His laugh was dry. 'I'm not into you yet, Alice. But I'm
hoping I will be soon.'

Jeremy was mightily relieved when she crawled back up
onto his chest and kissed him, on the mouth this time.
He wound his arms round her without thinking, his heart
lurching as he held her naked body tightly against his.
How brave she was, he thought. And how sexy. He could
not get enough of her.

When she sat up and straddled him across his thighs, he
sighed in relief. But when she reached over and opened a
bedside drawer, extracting a box of condoms, it struck him
just how prepared she'd been for tonight's outcome. Maybe
not for the being-on-top part, but for having sex with him.
Perversely, Jeremy found himself feeling slightly offended.
A crazy reaction, given the circumstances. But it was no
use. He hated the idea that he might be just the means to
an end for Alice. Yes, she fancied him. That much was obvious. But what would happen afterwards? Would she roll
off him and say, *Thank you very much, Jeremy dear, but
you can go now. Your job is done*?

'I'm sorry,' she said suddenly after tearing open one of the foil packets. 'I don't think I can manage. I mean…it looks so small and you're so big.'

'My size is average,' he said more sharply than he intended. 'Erections tend to be large when the man is as turned on as I am. Here! Give it to me.'

He rolled the condom over himself with the speed afforded by lots of practice.

'Heavens,' she said. 'That was impressively quick.'

Jeremy prayed for patience. 'Could we possibly move on, please?' he bit out through gritted teeth.

The heartbreakingly hesitant look she gave him quashed his anger. But did little to quell his rampant desire for her.

'I'm n-not sure what to do next,' she said.

'Go up on your knees,' he told her. 'Take me in your hands and push me inside a little, then hold it firmly at the root as you lower yourself gently onto me.'

She did as he said, the concentration on her face broken by a sudden gasp. Whether it was pain or pleasure he wasn't sure. On his part he thought she felt fantastic. Tight and wet and delicious.

'Are you all right?' he asked whilst he clenched his jaw in an attempt to gain control of his flesh. Lord, but he was already close to disaster.

'Yes,' she replied somewhat shakily. 'Fine. It feels fine. No, it feels more than fine. Oh, God, it feels fantastic.'

I'm not an it, he wanted to throw at her. *I'm a him. A person. A man.*

She began rocking to and fro, then rising up and down, riding him, killing him. He groaned, aware of hot blood rushing through his veins. Hell, he was only seconds from coming. Fortunately, she came first, throwing her head back as her mouth gaped open and a keening cry erupted from her lips. His release followed instantly, their bodies shuddering as one, Jeremy having not felt an orgasm like that in his life, his physical satisfaction overlaid by a most uncharacteristic emotional response.

Jeremy almost panicked—falling in love with Alice was *not* on his agenda—but he finally realised that his feeling of intense satisfaction was connected with being Alice's first lover, plus happiness over the fact she'd found the experience so pleasurable. He doubted many girls had screaming orgasms during their initiation into sex. Not that he could take too much credit for that. His male ego was suffering from an underlying irritation that he hadn't exactly done much to achieve that. Just lain there and let her use his body.

Next time, he vowed, it was not going to be like that.

'Absolutely not,' he muttered under his breath when she collapsed across him, his arms encircling her still-panting body with a fierce possessiveness. He definitely would not be letting her dismiss him afterwards, either, as if he were just a convenient piece of meat. He would not rest till she agreed to a lot more than this one time.

Alice lay across Jeremy's chest, wallowing in the security of his arms whilst trying to come to terms with what had just happened. She'd always suspected she would enjoy sex, if she could learn to trust a man enough. And now that she'd experienced the real thing, she wanted to experience more of it. But not with other men. With Jeremy. He was the one she wanted. He was the one she…

Alice caught herself up short before she even thought that dreaded word. She didn't love Jeremy. *Could* not love him. He didn't want her to. And really, she didn't want to, either. He was a playboy, a confirmed bachelor who changed women as often as he changed his clothes. Which was pretty often. She hadn't seen him in the same outfit or suit since they'd met.

'Everything okay?' he murmured into her hair.

'Yes. Yes, I'm good.'

'You might be a little sore tomorrow.'

Her head lifted and she smiled down at him. 'How would you know? You don't do virgins. Till tonight, that is.'

He gave a narrow-eyed glance. 'I have had many female friends over the years. Women like to talk. The things I know about the opposite sex would surprise you.'

'Nothing you know about the opposite sex would surprise me, Jeremy,' she said as she dropped her head back down on his chest.

'That didn't sound like a compliment.'

'It wasn't a criticism, either. Just a fact.'

'So where do we go from here, Alice?' he asked her.

Her head lifted again. 'What do you mean?'

'I sincerely hope you're not going to tell me that this is it—that my job is done and it's *hasta la vista*, baby. Whilst I might have had the odd one-night stand in the past, that's not what I want with you, Alice.'

'What do you want, then?'

'I want you to be my girlfriend.'

Alice swallowed. This was dangerous territory here. 'For how long?'

'Who knows? For as long as it lasts, I guess.'

'As what lasts?'

'Our lust for each other.'

'You think that's all it is between us? Lust?'

'Not on my part. I like you as well. I don't just want to take you to bed, Alice. I want to take you out. To show you how to have fun. I think you need that. But I'm going to be brutally honest. In my experience, once the lust begins to fade—and it always does eventually—then the liking soon follows.'

'I see. Well, I wouldn't know about that. I've never been in lust before. So how often would you be wanting to take me out?'

'I would imagine every weekend. And perhaps at least

once during the week. I'd certainly like to see you again fairly soon. I want to make love to *you* next time, Alice.'

Alice's mouth dried at the thought. She could hardly wait. But feminine instinct warned her that to be too eager would be the kiss of death with Jeremy. It might be the kiss of death with her, too. She suspected that if the next time was as marvellous as this first time, it wouldn't be long before she fell in love with this man. She didn't want that. It would be the height of foolishness. If truth be told, she should finish things right here and now. But she simply could not. At the same time, she vowed to keep some control over their relationship.

'I don't know about becoming your girlfriend, Jeremy. Could we just be friends and lovers? Neither of us are interested in marriage, or commitment for that matter, so I think it's best we don't pretend differently.'

His frown showed some displeasure with her counter suggestion.

'I would not want you dating anyone else whilst you're dating me,' he said.

She tried not to look as thrilled as she felt. 'The same goes for me.'

'Good. So when will I see you next? Tomorrow night?'

As much as she wanted to, she feared that having Jeremy make love to her so soon might see her getting way too emotionally involved way too quickly. Fortunately, she had a legitimate reason to delay things. 'Sorry, but I'll have to say no. Like you said, I might be sore tomorrow. On top of that, my period is due in the afternoon and I'm as regular as clockwork.'

Jeremy sighed. 'I see. So how long does your period last?'

'I should be right by Thursday.'

'Damn. I have to go to Paris on Thursday. I'm trying to set up an office there but the woman I wanted to head the place has taken a job elsewhere. I have to interview some new applicants for the job.'

'You speak French?'

'Passably.'

Alice lowered her head back to his chest. 'I'm hopeless with languages.'

'You'll still come to New York with me next weekend?' he asked, one hand trailing tenderly up and down her spine.

She sighed with a mixture of pleasure and resignation. 'Yes, of course. I can't wait.'

'Me too. Look, the rain's stopped so I think I'd better go.'

She sat up abruptly and pushed back her messy hair with both hands. 'But why? You haven't had dessert yet and I made a peach pie.'

He laughed. 'If I stay, *you're* the one who'll be my dessert, sore or not. Now don't look at me like that. I've done the job you asked me to do. Time for me to go.'

Guilt saw her flushing. 'I never meant it to sound like that. I was just trying to be pragmatic about everything. I thought you would prefer it that way. I knew you wouldn't want hearts and flowers.'

'You're the one who didn't want flowers,' he pointed out. 'I'm not averse to a little romance occasionally.'

'Sorry. I've been a bit screwed up.'

'And you're not screwed up now?'

Only in so far as I might already *be falling in love with you*...

'I think I'm going to be a normal girl from now on,' she pronounced.

His blue eyes narrowed. 'Normal how? You won't start wanting a ring on your finger, will you?'

'Not in the near future,' she said. 'And not with you, Jeremy. You've made your position quite clear.'

'Good. Now I'll be off. I'll ring you tomorrow. If we can't have sex, we can at least talk.'

She stayed naked whilst he dressed, shamelessly ogling

him as he did so. What a gorgeous body he had. Broad shoulders. Flat stomach. Slim hips. Great skin. And a penis to die for. He was wrong about his size. He wasn't obscenely huge but he *was* above average. Of course, Jeremy was above average in every department. He was smarter and kinder, and he could kick butt like Alice could hardly believe. She would always feel safe around him. She *did* feel safe. And strangely loved. She knew he didn't actually love her but he liked her enormously. And he cared about her. That was obvious.

Once he was dressed he bent to give her a long lingering kiss. 'Talk to you tomorrow,' he said when his head finally lifted.

'Jeremy…'

'Yes?'

'Thank you.'

His smile had an odd edge to it. 'My pleasure.'

Alice wondered afterwards what it had meant. That smile. In the end she decided she didn't want to know. She would enjoy whatever time she had with Jeremy, without regrets. She would be wretched when he moved on, but she would survive. Somehow. Tonight, he'd given her the tools to survive. He'd made her feel normal.

CHAPTER EIGHTEEN

NEW YORK. IN a few minutes she'd be in New York. With Jeremy.

Alice's stomach tightened with pleasurable anticipation. She wasn't sure what excited her the most. Going to the red-carpet premiere of *An Angel in New York*, or spending a whole night with Jeremy. In a five-star honeymoon suite no less!

Having to wait a week before they could make love again had increased her desire for him to fever pitch, all his long chatty, caring phone calls making her fall for him with a dizzying depth that could not be denied any longer. Silly to keep denying it, at least to herself. Given Jeremy's playboy history, it would have been better if she'd been the type of girl who could enjoy a strictly sexual fling without emotional involvement. But she hadn't been made that way, had she?

Still, she wouldn't worry about that right now, turning her head and smiling over at him.

God, but he was gorgeous. Dressed in another suit, this one charcoal-grey, combined with a grey and white striped shirt and a bright gold tie. A rather bold choice but she loved it, as she loved him. And desired him. Tonight could not come soon enough.

Maybe you won't have to wait till tonight, came the heart-stopping thought. *It's only lunchtime. The premiere doesn't start till this evening*. They could spend the afternoon making love.

'What on earth are you thinking?' Jeremy suddenly asked.

'What? Oh, nothing important. Just working out how I'm going to do my hair for tonight.'

'You little liar,' he chided laughingly. 'You were thinking about sex, weren't you?'

Alice's heart sank, perhaps because he'd used the word sex and not making love. Was that all their being together meant to him? Sex?

She suppressed a sigh. Being in love could be self-destructive, she decided, forcing a smile back to her lips.

'Well, of course I'm thinking about sex,' she said. 'Having discovered the joys of the flesh, I'm keen for some further education under your expert hands.'

For some reason her breezy answer didn't please him, his eyes darkening with a definite cloud of annoyance. 'Really?' he said in mocking tones. 'Well, I would hate to disappoint you. I've never coveted the role of sexual tutor. But there's a first time for everything, I guess.'

Alice frowned, his cutting tone having put a dampener on her excitement.

You bastard, Jeremy thought as he saw the light go out in her eyes. *Why do that to her, just because of your own crazy mixed-up feelings? Of course she wants more sex, her naturally high libido having being released after all those years of enforced celibacy. Don't be such a louse. Give her what she wants. And do it well. She deserves it.*

And she deserves a man a whole lot better than you!

Leaning over, he kissed her on the cheek. 'It will be my pleasure, beautiful,' he murmured in a slightly husky voice. 'We'll make love all afternoon, if that's what you want.' He lifted his head to smile down at her. 'It's certainly what *I* want. This past week has been sheer torture with missing you.'

'I missed you, too,' Alice said, his sweet words restoring her happiness in a flash.

Getting through Customs took a while, but Alice didn't care as long as Jeremy was holding her hand—which he was—and giving her those smouldering, desire-filled glances. He might not love her but he certainly wanted her. That would have to do for now.

When they finally emerged into the terminal, wheeling their luggage, Sergio was waiting for them with a big grin on his handsome Italian face. Alice knew it was Sergio because he called Jeremy's name out before striding over and drawing his friend into a big bear hug, slapping him on the back whilst giving her a raised-eyebrow glance over Jeremy's shoulder.

'*Dio*, but I have missed you!' Sergio boomed.

Jeremy's expression was classic Jeremy. 'Good God, you've gone all Italian again.'

Sergio laughed. 'But I *am* Italian, my friend.'

'You weren't all those years you lived in London. You could have been taken for British.'

'Never. You are the British boy. And still a swanky dresser, I see. But something is different, I have noticed.' And he directed his eyes at Alice.

Jeremy whirled, looking sheepish. 'Sorry, Alice. I wasn't deliberately ignoring you.'

'It's perfectly all right, Jeremy,' she said with a warm smile. She had enjoyed seeing the two friends together, had found comfort in Jeremy's affection for his friend. He was capable of loving a person, then. 'So this is Sergio?' she said, coming forward and holding out her hand. 'I've heard a lot about you and your days at Oxford together.'

Sergio bypassed her outstretched hand and hugged her too. 'And I have not heard nearly enough about you,' he returned. 'But I am impressed, Jeremy. Alice is the kind of lady I always thought would be the perfect partner for you.'

Jeremy groaned. 'Watch it, Alice. He'll have us married off before you know it. Sergio used to be as committed a bachelor as myself but after he turned thirty-five the rot set in.'

'I don't think Bella would like being described as rot,'

Sergio retorted. 'Besides, you knew full well that I intended on marrying when I returned to Italy. I told you that my days as a member of the Bachelor Club were well and truly over.'

'What's the Bachelor Club?' Alice asked.

Sergio gave Jeremy a reproving look. 'You haven't told her about the Bachelor Club?'

Jeremy shrugged. 'It didn't seem necessary. After both you and Alex left, our little club was no more.'

'But you're still a member?' Sergio asked, casting another long glance at Alice.

'I am, despite being thirty-five.'

'What has thirty-five got to do with anything?' Alice asked, her curiosity piqued.

'It was the age we vowed to remain bachelors till,' Jeremy informed her. 'Perhaps we should go get a cab, Sergio. Alice is tired after the flight and needs to have a little lie-down before tonight.'

Alice sucked in a sharp breath. Still as wicked as ever, she conceded. And annoyingly enigmatic at times.

The ride from the airport into the city was slow and tedious, New York traffic on a par with London's. Thank heavens the taxi drivers were just as chatty as London cabbies. Theirs kept showing them points of interest, taking them for tourists. They didn't tell him otherwise. Finally, they arrived at their hotel, porters taking care of their luggage, Jeremy handling their check-in whilst Sergio stayed with Alice.

'How long have you known Jeremy?' he asked straight away.

Alice had to think for a moment. 'About three weeks,' she said, astonished that it was so short a time. It felt as if she'd known him for much longer than that.

'How did you first meet?' came his next question.

She told him the truth, about the charity auction, her fund-raising, her job, et cetera, believing that truth was always the best policy. Of course, she did omit some facts. Sergio didn't have to know the circumstances behind their becoming an item, letting him fill in the blanks, probably wrongly. Like Jeremy, he would never imagine she'd been a virgin till recently, or that Jeremy was her first lover.

'Jeremy's a good man,' Sergio said. 'But he's been damaged by that appalling family of his.'

'Yes, I know,' she said softly. 'But no more about that. He's coming back.'

'So he is. Glad to have met you, Alice. And to have this opportunity to talk to you. It's going to be busy tonight so I might not get another chance.'

'Chance to do what?' Jeremy asked as he joined them.

'To chat,' Sergio said. 'Have to go, I'm afraid. Hell, I almost forgot. I've hired a limousine to pick you up tonight at seven.'

'How very Hollywood of you,' Jeremy said laughingly.

'It's what you have to do. The media can make or break a movie and we all have money in the damned thing, you included.'

'Not as much as you, I'll warrant,' Jeremy said. 'Is it a good movie?'

'Haven't seen it yet. But Charlie says it's great.'

'He's Bella's agent, isn't he? You can't believe him.'

'Don't say things like that. I'm stressed enough as it is, keeping Bella calm and confident. Now I do have to go. See you tonight. Your seats are next to ours, but we have to be there before you. Photos and interviews. Ciao.'

'They won't take photos of us, will they?' Alice asked a bit anxiously after Sergio left.

'Possibly. But why the frown? You'll look beautiful as always.'

'I should have bought a new dress.'

'Rubbish. That black number is gorgeous. And not in any way cheap. It has designer label written all over it. I know my fashion, Alice.'

'It was Fiona's dress. She gave it to me.'

'Who cares? It will do perfectly.'

'I won't hold a candle to Bella.'

'You'll outshine her in my eyes.'

'Oh…' Alice's heart went to mush. 'You say the nicest things.'

'You make me a better man,' he quipped, then grinned. 'Come on. Let's go upstairs to our room.'

Of course, it wasn't just a room. It was the honeymoon suite. Five star and fabulous.

'This must be costing you a small fortune,' she said as she walked through the enormous sitting room then glanced into the opulent bathroom with its corner spa bath and shower built for three.

'I'm using the money I saved from not having to buy you an original ten-thousand-dollar gown to wear tonight, plus a diamond necklace to go with it. No, whoops. I lied about the necklace part.'

Alice's eyes almost popped out of her head when he whipped a black velvet case out of his jacket pocket and held it out to her.

'You are kidding me,' she said when she opened it and saw the most exquisite diamond necklace. A sinfully expensive choker, with three rows of diamonds whose sparkle was reflected in her suddenly bright eyes. 'They can't be real,' she added as she drew it out of the box with reverent fingers.

'They'd better be,' he said drily.

'You shouldn't buy me expensive gifts like this, Jeremy,' she chided.

'Why not?'

'I'm your friend, not your mistress.'

'Can't a man buy a friend gifts?'

'Not ones that cost as much as this. And if you say you can afford it, I'm going to hit you.'

'Not with that lethal weapon in your hands, I hope.'

Alice stared down at the gorgeous necklace some more, unable to hold on to the tinge of dismay which had accompanied his giving it to her.

'When did you buy it? In Paris?'

'No. I was too damn busy in Paris to go shopping.'

'Please don't tell me you had Madge buy it for you.'

'Lord no,' he said laughingly. 'She would have had us married off even quicker than Sergio. No, I have many connections, Alice, from my financial consultancy days. One of them is a jeweller. He showed me this online, let me have it wholesale and couriered it over to me yesterday evening. So you do like it?'

'Do I like it? I love it,' she said, clasping it close to her heart. *And I love you*, she added silently.

'I could have bought matching earrings but I thought the necklace was enough. Too much glitz would detract from your classy look. And your beauty.'

Tears pricked at her eyes, which alarmed him.

'You're not going to cry, are you?'

'Sorry.' She quickly blinked them away. 'It's been a long time since I've been given something so fabulous. Thank you, Jeremy.' And she came forward to peck him on the lips.

'Surely you can thank me better than that.'

She feigned confusion. 'What would you suggest?'

'A shower first, I think, then a little lie-down together when you can show me just how grateful you are.'

Very grateful, Jeremy was to think ruefully when they were in the shower together.

Her kisses were wildly passionate, her tongue as avid as his own. She didn't take much encouragement to go down on her knees before him. He tried to recapture his earlier resentment over his body being used by her, but it would not come. All he could think about was how incredible her lips felt, how much he wanted her to keep doing what she was doing.

And she did, shocking him with her quite wanton passion, forcing him to use every ounce of willpower he owned to stop her before she went all the way. For that was not what he wanted on this occasion. He wanted to make love to *her*, not the other way around. He wanted to make her desperate for him. Wanted to watch her come and come. Wanted to show her that she couldn't possibly have so many orgasms with any other man, that only he, Jeremy, could do that for her.

And when he couldn't stand it any more, he would allow the beast in him to take her in a way where she couldn't see his eyes, couldn't glimpse the depth of his feelings, feelings that scared the life out of him.

Alice lay back on the bed, her legs stretched wide, her eyes squeezed tightly shut as Jeremy did to her what she'd often fantasised about but never hoped to enjoy. How delicious it felt to be made love to that way. Totally decadently delicious.

'Eyes open, Alice,' he ordered thickly, and she did so.

'Now keep them open.'

Frustration brought a moan to her lips. He dropped his head again and soon she was twisting her own head from side to side, her mouth gasping wide, frantic hands clutching at the sheets. Her climax made her cry out, twisting at her insides, which felt oddly empty. Almost bereft. She thought he would stop then but he didn't. He kept going, licking, sucking, exploring, and soon that awful tension was gripping her once more. Awful this time because it was no longer what she wanted. But she felt powerless to stop her body from responding, unable to say no. She came again, her pleasure not nearly as sharp, or as satisfying.

When he continued, she simply could not bear it. 'No, Jeremy, no,' she begged. 'Enough.'

He slid back up her body and kissed her, making her taste herself on his lips. She could not believe how exciting she found that, how much she loved his tongue in her mouth. She moaned in dismay when he abandoned it to concentrate on her breasts, which felt swollen and heavy and, yes, eager for attention. He gave them that, and more, till her nipples were burning and she was once again pleading with him to stop. He shocked her then by turning her over and kissing her all the way down her spine to the cleft between her buttocks.

Panic churned her stomach at the thought that he might do something she didn't want him to do. But he didn't. After reaching for a condom, he pulled her up onto her hands and knees and entered her from behind, bringing a sigh of relief, and, yes, the most exquisite pleasure. How ready she was for him to do this, she thought as he moved inside her. How madly, marvellously ready. Her bottom pressed back hard against him, her breathing going haywire, her blown-away mind on nothing but the feel of his flesh filling hers.

'Oh, yes,' she cried out when he started rocking back and forth. 'Yes…'

His hands finding her aching breasts and plucking at her needy nipples tipped her immediately over the edge, a violent orgasm ripping right through her. He came too, roaring his release, his hands squeezing her breasts as his body shuddered into her own shuddering flesh. Alice collapsed onto the bed in a crumpled heap, Jeremy falling on top of her. And there they lay, chests heaving, hot breaths panting from their lungs till slowly, finally, the air stilled around them and the room fell quiet.

Alice surrendered to sleep first, Jeremy lying sprawled across her unconscious form for a long while before slowly withdrawing and heading for the bathroom.

CHAPTER NINETEEN

THE MOVIE WAS GOOD, Jeremy thought even before the credits started to roll. No, it was more than good. It was great. A winner. All total fantasy, Jeremy accepted, but enjoyable in a strictly escapist fashion, a feel-good movie in every way. The music was great too, the lyrics emotional and uplifting. Bella had sung most of the songs and she'd been incredibly good. Jeremy had heard her sing once before—at a royal gala performance in London—but she had outdone herself this time. His investment in the movie was safe. Not that he cared about that for himself. He hadn't put that much money in it. But he was glad for Sergio.

The audience stood up and started clapping at the end. When Jeremy turned to Alice, she had tears in her eyes. Women! Such emotional creatures. But if truth be told, he'd been touched himself by the story.

'Wasn't Bella wonderful?' she said as they made their way slowly down the aisle. 'And this theatre is amazing!'

The premiere had been held at the Paris theatre, the last remaining single auditorium theatre in New York and patron of independent movies. Built post war, it was not as opulent as other theatres of that era, but it still retained that air of old-fashioned elegance and glamour, with a magnificent velvet curtain covering the large curved screen and almost six hundred surprisingly comfortable leather seats.

Jeremy tapped Bella on her shoulder. She and Sergio were just in front of them.

'Alice said you were wonderful,' he told her. 'And you were. So was the movie.'

Bella stopped and turned, giving them both a warm smile. 'Thank you, Jeremy darling. And you, too, Alice. I know we haven't had the opportunity for girl talk yet but Sergio said you were just what the doctor ordered for Jeremy.'

Jeremy rolled his eyes. 'Enough of the matchmaking, Sergio. Alice and I are just good friends. Let's leave it at that for now.'

Bella gave him one of her intuitive looks. 'If you say so. You are coming to the after party, aren't you?'

'Wouldn't miss it for the world.'

The after party was held at Bella and Sergio's New York apartment, a splendid place, spacious and tastefully furnished. And a stone's throw from Broadway. Alice wasn't overawed—she'd been brought up around moneyed people—but she was amused by the antics of Bella's agents, Charlie and Josh. They were so over the top, and given to extravagant compliments. Within minutes of being introduced, they tried to sign Alice up, saying she was a wonderful cross between Grace Kelly and Audrey Hepburn—perhaps it was because she'd worn her hair up. Such a style plus Fiona's designer dress and Jeremy's fabulous necklace did give her a coolly sophisticated look. When she'd informed them she wasn't an aspiring actress but a counsellor, working with victims of domestic violence, they hadn't missed a beat, saying it would give her acting more depth to have had such tough life experiences. Unfortunately, at the time Jeremy was engaged talking to Sergio. Alice was relieved when Bella came to the rescue.

'Sorry, my darlings,' she said to her eager agents, 'but I need Alice here for a sec. Secret women's business,' she added before steering her away from the living room into a nearby bedroom, shutting the door firmly behind them.

'They can be a bit much, can't they?' Bella said.

'They mean well.'

Bella laughed. 'They are both greedy opportunists. And never to be trusted. But I can't blame them for pouncing on you. You are so lovely, and like a breath of fresh air after all the plastic wannabes which abound in our industry.'

'Well, *you're* nothing like that,' Alice said, thinking how exquisitely beautiful Bella looked in that one-shouldered white chiffon gown. Princess line, it was, with a long flowing skirt that brushed the floor. Her lovely face was made up perfectly, her long white-blonde hair cascading in gentle waves over her shoulders.

Her smile was a little wry. 'My looks have been a great asset but I hope my voice is what I am remembered for. But enough of that, I wanted to talk to you about Jeremy, and that silly Bachelor Club of theirs. Sergio tells me you didn't know anything about it.'

'No. Should I? I already know Jeremy is a confirmed bachelor.'

A frown formed on Bella's high forehead. 'And you're okay with that?'

Something unhappy must have shown on Alice's face.

'I didn't think you would be,' Bella said drily. 'You're in love with him, aren't you?'

'How...how can you tell?'

Bella shrugged. 'Most women fall in love with Jeremy. Fortunately, when I met him I was already besotted with Sergio, otherwise I might have surrendered to the spell of his wicked charm.'

Alice sighed. 'He does have a way about him.'

'But he won't marry you, Alice. Don't delude yourself into thinking he will.'

'I won't. Don't worry.' Though the horrid hope had briefly crossed her mind. 'Tell me about this Bachelor Club.'

'Look, it's just some silly club the three of them formed at Oxford. It had a whole lot of ridiculous rules. Mainly, they vowed to become billionaires by the time they turned thirty-five, and not to marry before then, either. They trundled along for years, making heaps of money and playing musical beds. It wasn't till they actually reached thirty-five and had achieved their financial goal that Sergio and Alex saw that it was crazy to block themselves off from the joy of true love. Sergio came looking for me and Alex found Harriet. But Jeremy seems trapped in his inability to open his heart to any woman. Sergio believes he's afraid of falling in love. Do you know about his family and all their divorces?'

'Yes, I do.'

'Well that's obviously the reason behind his playboy lifestyle. Maybe one day he'll realise that we all forge our own destinies in life—that we're not programmed to follow our parents' poor example. But I'm worried that before that happens, you are going to be very hurt.'

Her words moved Alice, as did her kindly concern. What a sweet woman she was.

Alice reached out and took Bella's hands in hers.

'It's all right, Bella,' she said. 'I'll be all right. I'm a survivor.' She'd had to be.

Bella shook her head. 'Then you're a lot tougher than I am. I don't know what I would have done if Sergio hadn't loved me back.'

How could he not have loved her back? She was so sweet and so lovable.

'Maybe Jeremy cares about me more than he knows,' Alice said with a sudden burst of optimism. 'He bought me this necklace. And he offered to buy me a house. Well, not for me personally. It was for the charity I started up to help abused women.'

Bella's eyes rounded. 'He did that for you?'

'Indeed he did.'

'Goodness. I'll have to tell Sergio. I'm sure he doesn't know. Maybe Jeremy is already changing. Love changes people, you know. Now we'd better get back before they send out a search party.'

'So where did you and Bella disappear to for a while?'

Jeremy asked in the taxi ride back to their hotel. It was very late, everyone having waited till the reviews came out on the movie. All had been positively glowing.

'Oh, she was having trouble with the zipper on her dress,' Alice invented. 'It took some time to fix.'

Jeremy nodded. 'That's because she's pregnant.'

Alice's head whipped round in surprise. 'She *is*?'

'Yes. Four and a half months. She didn't tell you?'

'No. Why would she? I'm not a relative, or a special friend. But that's great. She must be very happy.'

'Sergio's over the moon. It's a boy, according to the ultrasound.'

'I can't imagine a man like Sergio caring whether it's a boy or a girl, provided the baby is healthy.'

'True. He's one in a million, Sergio. The best friend a man could have.' Jeremy sighed. 'I just wish that he didn't live in Italy. Though speaking of Italy, he's invited us to visit them one weekend at his villa on Lake Como. Would you like that?'

'I'd love it,' she said, her heart dancing with happiness.

'Good. Then we'll go in July. Lake Como in the middle of summer is perfect.'

July was two months away, Alice thought. Which meant Jeremy didn't anticipate their relationship ending before then. Maybe it would never end. Maybe one day he'd confess he'd fallen in love with her and ask her to marry him.

And maybe pigs would start falling out of the sky.

But as she lay in his arms later that night, her body sated from more wonderful lovemaking, Alice's mind kept plaguing her with the romantic fantasy of their being married, and having a baby of their own. Astonishing thoughts, really, given the people involved. Jeremy hadn't been the only one who'd spent their life up till now not wanting marriage. Alice had always believed she'd never trust a man enough with her body to contemplate such a union. The fact that she trusted Jeremy enough to consider putting her happiness in his hands was truly amazing. Was it the blindness of her own love that inspired such optimism?

Possibly.

Probably.

As she finally drifted off to sleep she kept thinking of what Bella had said. How she was afraid that one day Jeremy was going to hurt her. Terribly.

CHAPTER TWENTY

'I CAN'T BELIEVE you and Jeremy are still seeing each other,' Fiona said over breakfast that Monday morning. 'I mean, it's been over a month now, hasn't it?'

'Six weeks actually,' Alice said. May had given way to June, summer having arrived in London, along with the humidity and the tourists.

Fiona shook her head. 'Amazing. It's not like him at all. And not like you either, sweetie. Of course, he *is* pretty irresistible. Even I can see that. But do try not to get too carried away. Or start thinking he'll marry you because he won't. And speaking of marriage, I'll be sending out my wedding invitations this week and I wondered what I should put on yours. Perhaps Alice Waterhouse and partner would be best, don't you think? After all, you and Jeremy might not be together by late August.'

Alice had a faint suspicion that Fiona was slightly jealous of her relationship with Jeremy, and was looking forward to the moment it failed. Her own fiancé wasn't nearly as handsome as Jeremy, or as nice. If truth be told Alistair was a right royal snob and so were his parents. Alice didn't envy Fiona one bit.

'Alice and partner would be fine,' Alice replied. 'Oh, and, Fiona, I'll be moving out soon.'

'You're not going to move in with Jeremy, are you?'

'No.' Though she practically lived at his place, spending every weekend and several nights during the week there. 'I've saved the deposit for a flat of my own and I found one I rather liked yesterday.'

'Really? Where is it?'

'In Chelsea.'

'Chelsea! Can you afford a flat in Chelsea?'

'Yes. It only has one bedroom, but it's on the ground floor and has a nice little courtyard.' She didn't add that Jeremy's father's bank was footing the mortgage with her paying only the smallest interest. Fiona seemed put out as it was.

'But I was going to ask you to take over this place when I got married,' Fiona said snippily. 'I wouldn't have charged you too much. And you could have had a flatmate to share the cost.'

'I'm sorry, Fiona. I'm grateful for all you've done for me, but it's time I had a place of my own.'

Fiona sighed. 'I'm going to miss you, sweetie.'

But not too much or for too long, Alice accepted. She'd imagined they were close friends, but not close enough, apparently, for Fiona to ask her to be a bridesmaid. Yet she was having six.

Alice's phone ringing stopped this increasingly irritating conversation in its tracks. She imagined it was Jeremy. They were constantly on the phone with each other.

But it wasn't Jeremy. It was her mother.

'Hello, Mother,' an astonished Alice answered, standing up and heading to her bedroom for some privacy. She hadn't seen or spoken to her mother since last Christmas, their relationship still strained, despite the departure of Marigold's husband. Alice had only gone home at Christmas because it was the done thing. Plus, she'd wanted to see her nephew. Her sister, she'd long lost patience with. The sight of Marigold weeping over her husband's grave last year had turned her stomach. 'What's happened?' she asked, instant worry in her voice. 'Is Dickie all right?'

Her mother's sigh was audible down the line. 'Dickie is fine. I've rung to tell you that your sister has become engaged and wants you to meet her fiancé. We're having a small family celebration this Saturday night. Not a party.

Jarod didn't want that. Just dinner and a cake. So can you come? *Will* you come?' she amended.

Alice took a few moments to assemble her thoughts, shock at this news having rendered her temporarily speechless.

'Who's this Jarod?' were her first words. 'Where on earth did Marigold meet him?'

'He's one of the gardeners she employed to landscape the grounds.'

A gardener. Alice could not believe it. First, Marigold married an abusive billionaire. Then, when she should have been old enough to know better, she got herself seduced by a possible gold-digger.

'Now don't jump to conclusions, Alice. You have a habit of doing that. Jarod's not after her money. He really loves her. And she loves him.'

I'll be the judge of that, she thought angrily.

'So will you come?' her mother asked somewhat tentatively.

'Wild horses wouldn't keep me away,' Alice bit out.

'Excellent. I'll see you Saturday, then. Let me know what train you'll be on and I'll have someone meet you at the station.'

Alice hesitated for a moment, then said, 'I won't be coming by train. I'll be driving down.'

'You've bought a car?'

'No. I... I've got myself a boyfriend.' Oh, Lord. Jeremy would hate being called her boyfriend. He'd probably hate taking her to a family function as well. Hopefully, he'd do it for her, if she asked nicely, because the thought of going alone was horrendous.

'A boyfriend!' her mother exclaimed. 'At last! Oh, Alice, I'm so pleased. Who is he?'

'His name is Jeremy Barker-Whittle.'

'Not one of *the* Barker-Whittles, is he? The banking dynasty?'

Trust her mother to know the names of every family in Britain with money. 'His family is in banking, yes. But Jeremy is in books. He's a publisher.'

'A publisher. How exciting! I love books.'

'Then you'll have plenty to talk about. It is all right that I bring him, then?'

'Of course. I'll put you both in the blue room.'

'Really, Mother? And if I asked for separate bedrooms?'

'Are you?'

'No.'

'Good. That pleases me even more.'

Alice just shook her head. She would never understand her mother.

'See you Saturday,' she said, and hung up, thankful that she didn't have to explain that conversation to Fiona. But she rang Jeremy immediately, unable to keep such news to herself. She caught him just before he left for work.

'I have some appalling news to tell you,' she said straight away.

'You're pregnant.'

'Don't be ridiculous. Of course not. I'm on the pill and you've been using condoms. Though you can throw them away now. The unsafe month is up.'

'And you call that appalling news?' he said laughingly.

'That's not it. Marigold is getting married. To a gardener, no less.'

'At the risk of calling you a snob, Alice love, what's so terrible about that?'

'Nothing. And I'm not a snob. But I just know he's after her money.'

'Ah. That old lack of trust in men raises its ugly head again.'

'Her husband's only been dead a year!' she protested.

'A husband she couldn't have loved,' Jeremy pointed out.

'She cried over his coffin.'

'They were probably tears of relief.'

'I thought you would understand,' Alice wailed.

'I do understand, my darling,' he said gently. 'You have every right to be wary for your sister. You love her. Look, I'll have a background check done on him. See if he has a criminal history. And I'll check out his financial status. Would that make you feel better?'

'Oh, yes, it definitely would. And, Jeremy...'

'Yes?'

'They're having a small celebratory dinner at home next Saturday night. Unfortunately, I opened my big mouth and asked if I could bring my new boyfriend with me. Sorry.'

'I see,' he said, not sounding too put out. 'Am I to presume you meant me?'

'Who else? So would you take me? *Please?*'

'Of course,' he agreed in that wonderfully easy-going way that she adored.

'You are so good to me,' she said with a soft sigh.

'It's easy to be good to someone like you, Alice.'

She almost told him then that she loved him. But she didn't, knowing instinctively that Jeremy didn't want to hear words of love. But she had no doubt in her heart that he knew she loved him, and that possibly he almost loved her back. He showed it all the time. Actions could be louder than words. Alice hugged that positive thought to herself.

CHAPTER TWENTY-ONE

WHEN JEREMY PICKED up Alice the following Saturday afternoon, the weather was humid, but drizzly. Alice, he saw straight away, looked beautiful but tense.

As soon as she was buckled up in the passenger seat, he handed her an A4-sized envelope.

'When you read that,' he said, 'you might feel better. It's the background check on Marigold's fiancé, as promised.'

'You were able to get it done in time!' she said with a relieved smile. 'You said it might be hard, given you didn't know this Jarod's surname.' Only because she'd refused to ring and ask.

'I called in a favour,' he replied, thinking of how small the world was. It turned out that the security firm he'd contacted to do the investigation was being managed by the very boy he'd saved from being bullied at school. Once Graham had found out his saviour was his new client, he had pulled out all stops to get the information Jeremy had wanted by this morning. But it had cost him a packet. Jeremy had refused Graham's offer of no fee, not wanting to take advantage of the man's gratitude.

Alice shook her head at him, though her expression was admiring. 'You are such a clever man.' Without further ado she ripped open the envelope.

Jeremy concentrated on getting out of London whilst Alice read the report, her occasional murmur of surprise pleasing him no end. He'd read the report himself, of course, and had been relieved to find out that Jarod Adams—that was his surname—was not some fortune-hunter. He actually owned more than three landscaping businesses and several nurseries. A self-made man, he had many millions in his bank, and many properties in his business portfolio, including a town house in Richmond and a seaside apartment in Brighton. Whilst having been born poor, he'd worked long and hard to get where he was today. He had no criminal convictions against his name, and his reputation was spotless. His employees couldn't speak highly enough of him. He was thirty-seven years old, six feet tall and very fit, according to the gym where he worked out. He had never been married. His parents had passed on, and his only sister lived in Australia.

'Not quite what you were imagining,' Jeremy said when her head finally lifted from her lap.

'No. He seems the real deal. Lucky Marigold. She deserves to be happy at long last.'

'Yes, she does, from what you've told me. So let's act happy for her when we arrive and not in any way suspicious. And try to be nice to your mother. I know your relationship is strained. I'm not stupid. But nothing's to be gained by letting your feelings show.'

Alice dragged in a deep breath before letting it out slowly. It was all very well for Jeremy to say that, but the hurts ran deep.

'I wonder if you'd be so nonchalant if you had to go to another of *your* family's weddings,' she said.

'God, the mind boggles at such a thought.'

'See? You wouldn't be so pragmatic if that happened.'

'True. But it won't. I think even they've had enough of the divorce court.'

'Not every marriage ends in divorce, Jeremy,' she said, hating herself for even bringing up the subject. But it was impossible not to hope that one day Jeremy might get over his aversion to commitment. He loved her. She was surer now than ever that he did. He just refused to admit it. 'Your two best friends seem very happy in their marriages,' she pointed out quietly.

He slanted her an incisive glance. 'I hope you haven't changed your mind, Alice. You told me you weren't interested in marriage.'

Alice saw immediately that she'd backed herself into a corner. What to say? How to handle this?

Her shrug was brilliantly nonchalant. 'All I am saying is that not every marriage ends in the divorce court.'

'It does, if there's a Barker-Whittle involved. Just be happy with what we have, Alice. Don't spoil things by wishing for the moon. Our relationship works because we have our feet firmly on the ground. Marriage changes things. So does living together. Speaking of living arrangements, when are you going to move into your new flat? It will be good not to have Fiona hovering behind you every time I come to pick you up.'

Alice dared not look over at him, lest her dismay show in her eyes. She'd been half hoping that Jeremy might ask her to move in with him at some stage. If he'd loved her he would have. Clearly, his feelings didn't run that deep.

Her heart sank as she accepted that her foolish optimism where he was concerned was just that. Foolish. She'd known what he was when she became involved with him. She'd been well warned. It was a minor miracle that things had lasted this long.

'Should be in by the end of the month,' she said, striking what she hoped was the right common-sense tone. 'I'm really looking forward to it. I like my own space at times. Having my own place will be a dream come true.'

She was one independent woman, Jeremy thought irritably. He was glad now that he hadn't given in to that insane temptation this last week to ask her to rent out her flat and move in with him. After all, she would have only said no. Yes was not a word Alice was overly comfortable with. She did say yes quickly enough when she was turned on, but other than that she could be extremely difficult. In the end, she hadn't even let him contribute to the purchase of that house next door to the refuge, buying it instead with funds raised, the website Madge had designed bringing in lots of donations for her charity.

She did finally agree to let him pick her up at work when she stayed back late, but she still took the Tube during the day. Neither would she let him lavish her with designer clothes, choosing instead to scour the markets for once-expensive vintage dresses to wear when he took her out to the kind of society do he was always getting invited to. Not that she didn't always look beautiful. She did. But he liked buying her things. Liked spoiling her.

The possibility that he was falling in love with Alice continued to haunt him at times. But none more so than at this very moment. Jeremy had always known that his family was flawed when it came to love. They often fell hard and fast, made stupid decisions, then fell out again just as quickly, leading to shattered marriages and shattered children.

I will not be a party to that stupidity, he vowed. *Not even for Alice*. Not that she would want him to. Clearly, she wasn't in love with him. Women in love couldn't wait to tell you and she'd never mentioned that particular four-letter word. This realisation should have made him feel better but it didn't. Damn it, but he had to pull himself together here.

'Surprisingly little traffic,' he said once they were safely on the M3. 'The rain, no doubt,' he added, the earlier drizzle having become much heavier.

'I don't mind the rain,' Alice said. 'I like to lie in bed and listen to the rain.'

'I like to lie in bed with you,' he said. 'Will we be in the same bedroom tonight?'

'Yes. But be warned. As soon as my mother heard that you were a member of the Barker-Whittle banking dynasty, she whipped us into the best guest room together.'

Jeremy laughed. 'I could grow to like your mother.'

'Huh. You are going to behave yourself, I hope. No flirting with Marigold or trying to seduce my mother.'

'Spoilsport. How old is she?'

'Marigold is thirty-three.'

'I meant your mother.'

'She turned fifty-nine last month.'

'Still a spring chicken.'

'Jeremy, you are incorrigible.'

'And you are delightful when you're jealous. But you don't have any cause for worry, my darling. Since I met you, I haven't even looked at another woman.'

'I don't believe that for a minute.'

'Would I lie to you?'

'Yes,' she pronounced firmly.

The trip took almost three hours, with their stopping once for coffee on the way, Alice's tension over the night ahead returning as they drove up the long driveway to the home she'd never been happy living in after her father died. A Georgian mansion built eons ago, it sat on the top of a hill overlooking the coast, though the sea could only be glimpsed from the two upper floors. The outer walls were fawn, the windows white, the roof and chimneys terracotta. Inside, not counting the servants' quarters downstairs, there were eight bedrooms, five bathrooms, a huge ballroom, spacious receptions and dining rooms, and a magnificent oak staircase. Most of the furniture were genuine antiques, the massive amount of artwork having been collected over the centuries by every earl to inhabit Hilltop Manor.

The original estate had had many acres and farms, but a lot of land had been sold off to pay her father's debts. The furniture and artwork might have gone too, if Marigold hadn't found herself a rich husband, a self-made mobile phone magnate. As it turned out, Rupert had coveted the grandeur of the house with its aristocratic history and opulent decor, but he hadn't been much interested in the gardens, so the grounds had been badly neglected for years.

Not so now, Alice thought with wonder as the extent of work done since Christmas became obvious. An impressive circular gravel driveway now greeted guests as they arrived, along with a lovely fountain, which sparkled in the sunshine, the rain being left behind as they'd travelled further south. Red roses lined the rather plain front of the house, their blooms full and rich. To the right and left she could see that there'd been groups of trees planted, which, though still young, would one day provide wonderful shade, and a pleasant place to sit.

'Sergio's villa on Lake Como has a fountain,' Jeremy said as his car crunched to a halt next to the elegant front portico, which was framed by Corinthian pillars made from creamy white marble. 'But it's a little more...shall we say... provocative?'

'What do you mean? Provocative?'

His smile carried amusement. 'Difficult to describe. You will see for yourself when we go visit there soon. Sergio suggested next weekend. Would that suit you?'

'Yes, I suppose so.' She couldn't think about next weekend, with her mind totally on this weekend. On the here and now. Her breath caught when the heavy front doors were thrown open, and her sister emerged on the arm of a well-built, pleasant-faced man with thick brown hair and broad shoulders. Both were smiling, then laughing when little Dickie dashed between their legs and ran over to the passenger door.

'Auntie Allie's here, Auntie Allie's here!' he chorused, jumping up and down with childish glee.

'Wow,' Jeremy murmured. 'Wish I was as popular with Auntie Allie.'

'Don't be silly,' she threw at him. 'You know I'm crazy about you.' And she climbed out of the car to embrace her eager nephew.

* * *

I'm crazier about you, Jeremy thought as he too alighted. *Too crazy for my peace of mind.*

'Jeremy. Come and meet my sister and her fiancé,' Alice insisted, little Dickie already in her arms.

Marigold was not overly like Alice, either in looks or personality. She was pretty, yes, but a good few inches shorter, with curly strawberry-blonde hair, an ordinary mouth and blue-grey eyes. Her figure was very hourglass, with wide hips and a lush bosom. She was also a follower, he could see, forever glancing over at her beloved and looking to him for approval. He gave it, in spades, the man obviously in love. Jeremy wished them the best with warm words, but privately he was no less cynical than usual when it came to believing they were set for their happiness.

After introductions, the two men carried their luggage upstairs, the two sisters already chatting happily away behind them. Their mother, Marigold had informed Alice, was lying down with a migraine and wouldn't be joining the family till dinner, news that had inspired an eye-roll from Alice. Jeremy suspected that dinner could be tricky, resolving to use all his social skills to avert a possible disaster. They were here to celebrate Marigold's engagement, not settle old scores.

'Nanna's put you in the blue room,' an excited Dickie told Jeremy as they ascended the staircase. 'It's the biggest and bestest bedroom in the house.'

'I *am* privileged,' he replied with a warm smile. The child really was delightful. Almost made you want one for yourself. Jeremy immediately thought of his two friends' sons, a pang of uncharacteristic envy twisting his heart.

'What does privileged mean, Auntie Allie?' Dickie asked Alice.

'It means lucky,' she replied. 'Jeremy's a lucky man and you're a lucky boy.'

'Very lucky,' Jeremy murmured an hour later when they

were lying, replete, in each other's arms on top of the four-poster bed with its blue satin quilt and mountain of matching pillows. They'd begged off coming down for afternoon tea, both claiming weariness after the drive and the need for a shower and a nap before dinner this evening. Marigold had given them a surprisingly knowing look, making Jeremy revise his opinion of Alice's sister. Maybe she was smarter than she seemed.

'So what did you think of him?' Alice asked.

'I think Dickie is delightful,' he replied, tongue in cheek.

Alice punched him on the arm. 'You know who I mean.'

'I think Jarod's very much in love with your sister, and vice versa.'

'I do too. Gosh, but it's a relief. I was so worried. You know, Jeremy, it wasn't till I arrived here today that I realised just how much I do love my sister. When I saw her looking so happy, I just melted inside.'

'Mmm, yes, you do seem somewhat melted,' Jeremy said, his hands wandering into nicely moist places.

'Will you just stop that and let me talk for a while?'

'I'm not stopping you from talking. Please continue.'

Her sigh carried resignation to what he was doing. 'I can't think when you're doing that.'

'Then don't, Alice.'

She didn't.

CHAPTER TWENTY-TWO

ALICE SHOULD HAVE known that Jeremy would be a hit with her mother. But did he have to sit next to her at dinner, dragging his chair even closer so that Alice couldn't over-hear what they were talking about? With only five of them seated at a huge dining table, which could be extended to seat twenty, there was already a decent space between chairs. Dickie, of course, had long been put to bed. Alice chatted away with Marigold whilst her ears strained to catch what Jeremy was saying. With a voice like his, one would think that would be easy, but he could talk softly when he wanted to. It wasn't till the main course was whisked away and their glasses of wine were being re-plenished that Alice's mother spoke to her directly.

'Jeremy tells me that Kenneth Jacobs is one of his au-thors. He said that you'd met him, is that right?'

'Yes, we all had drinks and dinner together one night not long ago.'

'Oh, I do envy you both. I think he's an incredible au-thor. I'd love to meet him some day.'

'No reason why you can't,' Jeremy said. 'Do you ever come to London?'

'Not very often.'

'Then you should. This is a lovely home but it must get lonely living here at times.'

'Yes, it does,' she said with a sigh.

'Let me know when you want to come and you can stay at my place.'

'Oh!' Her mother actually blushed. 'How kind of you. I might just do that.'

* * *

'What in God's name were you doing asking my mother to stay at your place?' Alice snapped after she banged the door of the blue room shut around midnight, her temper finally getting the better of her. Or was it jealousy?

'Why shouldn't I ask your mother to stay?' he said in that annoyingly innocent way he could adopt at times. 'I was just trying to be nice.'

Her hands found her hips. 'Well, if you keep being that nice, she'll be booking us a church and reception place in no time. Is that what you want?'

'Hardly,' he replied. 'Look, I just felt sorry for the woman. Did you know how poor she was as a child?'

'Rubbish! She wasn't poor. Her family was old money.'

'Money which had dissipated over the years, due to death duties and poor investments. After the great depression there was nothing left but their warped pride. Then the war came, making matters even worse. In the end, her family was living in a crumbling old ruin, which had no electricity and very little furniture. Her mother became an alcoholic and her father succumbed to early dementia. *Your* mother had to leave school and get work in a local pub so they could eat.'

Alice stared at him in shock and disbelief. This was the first she'd heard of such things. 'How on earth do you know all this?' she demanded to know.

He shrugged. 'Women feel they can talk to me. They tell me things. Did you know Lily was working as a waitress when she caught your father's eye?'

So it was Lily already. Lord, but he was a fast worker. At the beginning of dinner he'd been addressing her as Lady Waterhouse. 'That's not true,' she countered sharply. 'Mother met my father at a New Year's Eve party, right here in this house.'

'She did. But she wasn't a guest. She was serving drinks.'

'If that's true, then why didn't she tell me? Why pretend she was part of the hoi polloi that night? I wouldn't have judged.'

'I don't know the answer to that. But I suspect Marigold knows. They seem very close.'

'They are,' Alice said with a sigh before falling silent for a full minute, her thoughts in a whirl. 'You know, Marigold told me tonight that Rupert wasn't nearly as bad as I'd imagined. She claimed he suffered from depression after his upbringing as a foster child and was prone to fits of uncontrollable anger. That was when he yelled at her and hit her. She assured me that after she fell pregnant with Dickie, he changed. He finally went to a doctor, got diagnosed as bipolar and started taking medication. Of course, by then I'd left home permanently so I didn't witness any such improvement. When I visited every Christmas I thought he was just pretending to be a good husband. Marigold claimed he'd really loved her and she loved him back. She said she knew his behaviour was unacceptable at times but she couldn't leave him because she'd been terrified he'd kill himself like our father did. When I asked her if she'd told Mother all this, she said she had, eventually, but she'd hidden the truth from her at first. When I'd made my fuss over his hitting her, Mother had actually come to Marigold for an explanation, Marigold saying I'd just overheard a lovers' spat and that it had been she who'd slapped Rupert, not the other way around. She said she was very convincing. So maybe Mother wasn't the monster I always thought.'

'She still shouldn't have sent you away to school.'

'Maybe she thought I needed to get away after Daddy's death,' Alice said with more insight into the situation. 'I was very much a Daddy's girl,' she went on rather wistfully. 'We would go riding together almost every day. He even took me to the races. I didn't know then that he was addicted to gambling. I thought it was all great fun and I loved him to death. When he killed himself I was beside myself with grief. It…it was a terrible time.' Guilt claimed Alice as she recalled blaming her mother for her father's death, screaming at her that it was all her fault; that she spent too much money on clothes and silly things like perfume and jewellery.

'I was pretty awful to my mother at the time,' Alice said sadly. 'It's no wonder she doesn't like me.'

'Don't be silly,' Jeremy said as he drew her into his arm and stroked her hair. 'Your mother loves you very much. She told me so. Reading between the lines, I think she's also very guilty over not believing you where Marigold's husband was concerned. Still, perhaps now you can understand why she was tempted to turn a blind eye. She must have been in a panic after your father died, bankrupt and in debt. To suddenly be poor again would have been her worst nightmare. Then along comes a white knight to seemingly rescue everyone, so she didn't want to hear what you had to say. Not that that makes it right. It wasn't right. She should have listened to you. But I think she's sorry. She said how happy she was to see you so happy. She's also very lonely, Alice. Maybe she'll meet someone if she comes to London and gets out and about.'

Alice pulled out of Jeremy's arms to stare up at him. 'You're not going to try to fix her up with Ken, are you?'

'Good God no, he's already fixed up with Madge.'

'He is?'

'Didn't I tell you?' he said as he wandered over to pick up his phone, which he'd left behind on a bedside table.

'No, you didn't.'

'Well, I'm telling you now,' he said as he checked his messages. 'I… Oh, no!' he groaned. 'I don't believe it. Hell, are they insane?'

CHAPTER TWENTY-THREE

'YOU DIDN'T HAVE to come with me,' Jeremy growled as he drove away from Hilltop Manor after breakfast the next morning. 'I could have picked you up on my way back. It's not as though I'll be staying there very long.'

Alice shot him a worried look. She'd never seen him like this, simmering away with a barely held fury, which she feared was about to explode. She didn't trust him to drive properly if she wasn't with him. And she certainly didn't trust him not to say unforgivable things to his parents.

Clearly, the news last night that they were back together again—with the full intention of remarrying once their respective divorces were finalised—did not sit well with Jeremy. After reading the message from his father, he'd thrown the phone down and begun pacing the room, enlightening Alice as to the situation in a painfully caustic tone, deriding both his parents as romantic fools if they thought this marriage would work any better than it had the first time round. Alice had been unable to make him calm down. Or to make him see sense.

'You can't control other people's lives,' she'd said to him at one stage. 'And who knows? Maybe it *will* work this time. Maybe they've always loved each other, underneath, but lost their way, as people do sometimes.'

He'd ground to an angry halt before spearing her with a savage look. 'If you honestly think that then you're as big a romantic fool as they are.'

That had hurt. It still hurt. But there was no use telling Jeremy that. He was hurting too, old tapes having risen to distress him to a degree that had shocked her. She hadn't realised till then just how badly his parents' initial divorce had affected him. Silly of her when she'd studied abandonment issues and the emotional damage associated with them. It confirmed her earlier opinion that Jeremy's becoming a playboy was a direct result of the misery he'd felt all those years ago, his life motto being better not to love at all if it didn't ever last.

Maybe she *was* a romantic fool for thinking that he might have finally fallen in love. With her. But she did. Alice glanced over at the bleak set of his face and wished with all her heart that she could tell him that she loved him; that she would never not love him.

But she didn't dare. Not right at this fraught moment.

'I want you to stay in the car when we get there,' came his harsh edict. 'Like I said, I won't be long. Ten, fifteen minutes max. Just long enough to tell them what I think of this marriage. And of them. It's way past time that they heard the unvarnished truth. Winston and Sebastian won't dare in case they get cut out of the will. I don't give a damn about Father's money. Frankly, I couldn't care less if I never set eyes on either of them from this day forth.'

'That's the biggest load of old rubbish I've ever heard,' Alice said with deceptive calm. As a counsellor she'd perfected sounding calm when sometimes she was anything but.

'What?' he said, his head whipping round so he could glower at her.

'You heard me, Jeremy. The reason you're so upset with them is *because* you love them.'

'*Love* them?' he spat as he headed for an exit off the main road. 'I don't love them. I *despise* them. Why, they'd have to be the most selfish, shallow, superficial human beings I have ever come across. They have no concept of true caring, or commitment. They only had children as a reflection of their own egos. At least they can't do that this second time round. They're too damn old!'

With that pronouncement, he stopped the car briefly at

a Give Way sign before turning left and speeding down a narrow curving road. Alice held her breath as the tyres screeched on the first corner. Fortunately, this did make Jeremy slow down a little.

'If you despise them so much,' she said, still in that same calm tone, 'then why have you chosen to emulate them?'

'What in hell are you talking about, woman? I'm as different from them as I could possibly be.'

'Really? Before I met you, Jeremy, I was warned that you were selfish and shallow and superficial, with no concept of true caring and commitment.'

He stared over at her. And it was whilst he was staring over at her that a lorry pulled out of a hidden driveway on their left. Alice screamed out, Jeremy swearing and slamming his foot on the brake. The car went into a side slew, clipping the front of the lorry with a force that sent it catapulting into the air, his door ricocheting off the trunk of a tree before landing on its passenger side, in a ditch.

Thank God for airbags, Jeremy thought dazedly, then glanced over at Alice.

She was still and silent. *Too* still and silent, her pale face pressed against an airbag.

'Oh, God, *Alice*!' he cried out. 'Are you all right? Speak to me, Alice!'

She didn't speak. But she did make a slight moaning sound. Not dead, came the gut-wrenching realisation. Dear heaven, if she'd been dead he would not have wanted to live. But what if she still died? What if…?

Suddenly, someone was knocking on his broken window.

'Are you all right, mate?' the man shouted.

'Yes. But my girlfriend's unconscious. Call an ambulance, will you?'

'Will do.'

Jeremy tried to get out but his door was jammed. He

could do nothing but wait till the emergency services arrived. He tried not to think of what Alice had said to him just before the accident, but how could he not think about her final words? Because they were true. So true. Till he met her, that was. Meeting Alice changed him. Made him nicer, kinder, less selfish and shallow. He'd even started secretly wanting what Alex and Sergio had. True love. And marriage. Even children. Yes, children. Children he would cherish and never send away to damned boarding school.

But none of that would happen if Alice died.

Why in God's name hadn't he told her he loved her before this; that he wanted more than their just being friends and lovers? Anyone could see that she probably loved him. She hadn't said so because he'd told her that he didn't want her love.

Jeremy groaned as despair filled his soul.

In the end, he closed his eyes and prayed.

CHAPTER TWENTY-FOUR

'CAN I GET you something, Jeremy?' the middle-aged nurse asked kindly. 'Coffee perhaps?'

'What? Oh, no. No, thanks. I had some earlier.' He hadn't, but he didn't want to have to leave Alice's side to go to the bathroom. Not now when she might wake up at any moment. He'd allowed Madge to drag him away on other nights after the doctors told him that they were putting Alice in an induced coma for a few days after her surgery to alleviate the swelling in her brain. She'd hit her head on the roof of the car during the accident, causing a depressed fracture of her skull, fluid forming to protect the brain. Too much fluid, unfortunately.

She'd never been on the critical list, but no one could convince Jeremy she wasn't in imminent danger of dying. The thought that he might still lose her—and that it was all his own stupid fault—tortured his mind whenever he was away from her bedside. So he was always back first thing the next morning, sitting with Alice all day, the kindly staff bringing his drinks and food. He still lost weight, his eyes sinking into his head. For the first time in his life, Jeremy looked every day of his thirty-five years, and more.

He wasn't aware of how worried everyone was about him. His parents had been aghast at his appearance. So were his brothers. Marigold and her mother had been equally shocked when they'd visited each day, having driven to London and booked into a hotel close to the hospital. Madge, of course, had acted with her usual common sense, taking him in hand and insisting that he go home every night where she made him some hot chocolate before putting him to bed. She even laid out fresh clothes for him in the bathroom, having discovered that he'd lost interest in clothes and would have worn the same ones the next day if she'd left them there on the floor where he dropped them. Most days, he didn't even shave.

When she'd tried to take him home tonight, however, Jeremy had been firm in refusing, because this afternoon they'd stopped doing whatever it was they were doing to keep Alice asleep, informing Jeremy that she should start coming out of her coma within the next twenty-four hours.

'Why don't you go home and have a sleep?' the nurse continued. 'The doctor said Alice won't wake up till tomorrow morning at least.'

Jeremy glanced at the wall clock. It was five past twelve. 'Well, it *is* tomorrow morning,' he pointed out with a small smile. 'So I'll stay here, if you don't mind.'

Here was a green vinyl armchair in which he'd sat every day for the past six days, watching Alice lying there with tubes entering and exiting her body.

'I have to go do my rounds,' the nurse said gently. 'Just press the buzzer if you need anything or you notice any change.'

Jeremy nodded, glad to be left alone with Alice. He wanted to talk to her out loud, tell her things that he hoped she might hear. He'd read where people in comas could hear more than people realised. Drawing the armchair closer to the bed, he picked up her left hand and held it gently within both of his.

'You're going to wake up soon, Alice,' he murmured. 'And you're going to be all right.' He gulped at the memory of the doctors saying they didn't anticipate any brain damage. God help them if they were wrong. 'First of all I want to say how sorry I am for the way I acted that day. If I hadn't been so damn irrational and childish then none of this would have happened. But in a weird kind of way, maybe good can come out of something bad. I still wish this had never happened, but it made me realise, my darling, just how much I love you. I tried to convince myself that I didn't, but it has been there for ages, in the back of my mind. You're in love with Alice, that voice kept telling me. You want to marry her. Can you imagine how Jeremy, the perennial playboy, reacted to that? It was untenable. Unthinkable! I took comfort in the fact that you said you didn't want marriage either. I thought I was safe. But you know what? I don't want to be safe any more. I would risk anything and everything to be with you, Alice. To live with you. Not as a lover but as your husband. I even want to have children with you. Is that amazing or what? Alex and Sergio are never going to believe it.'

The joy that dream evoked was quickly replaced by worry. 'But none of that is going to happen if I'm wrong and you don't love me back...'

Tears pricked at Jeremy's eyes at this most horrible thought. For what if she *didn't* love him back? What if he'd ruined everything with his stupidity and his insensitivity, his selfishness and, yes, his shallow attitude to life and love. He didn't deserve someone as wonderful as Alice; didn't deserve her love. Why *would* she love him? He was worse than his stupid parents. At least they were willing to give their love a second chance, whereas he'd just run away from it, like some coward.

Her fingers twitching against his sent Jeremy's eyes flying to her face. Was that a smile forming on her lips? Yes, yes, it was a definite smile. Her eyelashes fluttered, then slowly lifted, her gaze a little unfocused.

''Course I love you,' she croaked out before her eyelids closed again.

Jeremy dropped her hand and jumped up, forgetting all about the buzzer he was supposed to press and racing out into the corridor like some kind of demented idiot.

'She's awake!' he shouted out to the empty corridor. 'She's awake and she loves me!'

No one answered him, or heard him, so he bolted back

into Alice's room, found the buzzer in the bed and pressed it. The nurse came quickly, frowning when she saw the patient was sound asleep.

'Yes, what is it?' she asked in slightly harried tones.

'She woke up,' Jeremy told her. 'She spoke to me.'

The nurse sighed. 'Well, she's gone back to sleep now. Look, I suggest you go home and do the same. Nothing is to be achieved by this all-night vigil, you know. Don't you want to be all rested when your fiancée wakes up properly later today?'

'My fiancée?' he repeated, having forgotten that that was what he'd said to gain unlimited access to Alice's room.

'Yes, your fiancée,' the nurse said, not unkindly but knowingly. 'Perhaps a shave would be in order as well.'

Jeremy rubbed his hand across his three-day growth. 'A shave. Yes. You're right. Can't let Alice see me looking like this.'

'Good man. Now off you go. The hospital will let you know if there's any sudden change.'

Jeremy hurried off, resolving to do everything right this time. He'd been given a second chance with Alice and he wasn't about to waste it. Or waste time. He didn't go home straight away. Instead, after making a very important phone call, he drove into the city where a somewhat bemused jeweller showed up eventually to open up his store in the dead of night.

'Are you sure that's the one you want?' the man asked after Jeremy had paid for his selection. 'We have rings with bigger diamonds.'

'Alice wouldn't want anything too big, or too showy.' Not that the ring was cheap. The diamond was flawless, which meant it was expensive.

'Well, you know her better than I do. So are congratulations in order, Jeremy? This is an engagement ring you've just bought, after all.'

'I certainly hope so,' he said. 'But Alice has been known to say no to me.'

'I doubt she'll say no to this. Now, I will expect an invitation to the wedding,' the jeweller said as he locked up the shop.

Jeremy raced home with his precious purchase in his pocket. An hour later, he was back in the green vinyl chair, showered, shaved and dressed in his favourite grey suit. The nurse lifted her eyebrows at him when she came in around five to check Alice's vital signs.

'Well, you look a lot better,' she said. 'Nice bright tie. But I suspect you haven't had any sleep.'

'I dozed in this chair for a while.'

'Not enough. Still, I guess I'd do the same if I were in your shoes. You love Alice a lot, don't you?'

'More than I can say.'

'How romantic. So when are you going to ask her to marry you for real?'

'The second she wakes up.'

The nurse nodded, smiled, then left the room.

An hour later, Alice stirred. Jeremy didn't ring the buzzer, just held Alice's hand and waited, struggling all the while to contain his emotions.

I must not cry, he told himself. *I must not cry.*

Very slowly, her eyes opened, and this time her gaze was clear.

'Jeremy,' she said, smiling a sweet smile at him.

Jeremy swallowed. *I must not cry*, he repeated valiantly.

'How long have I been asleep?' she asked him.

'Six days,' he told her. And six long nights.

'That long. Where am I exactly?'

'In London. They flew you to this hospital when it became obvious you needed specialist care.'

'I see...and am I all right?' she asked, fear clouding her eyes.

'You banged your head in the accident. Cracked your skull. But yes, you're going to be fine.'

'That's good.'

'Do you want me to call for the nurse? Or the doctor?'

'No. Not yet. You know, I have this hazy memory of you talking to me and my saying something to you. Was I dreaming or did I talk to you during the night?'

'You did say something,' he admitted.

'What did I say?'

'You said you loved me.'

'Ooh. Oh, I see. Sorry. I know you don't want to hear things like that.'

'Don't be sorry. And I *do* want to hear it. Because I love *you*, Alice. I love you so much.' Knowing that actions always spoke more loudly than words, he reached into his jacket pocket and pulled out the ring box. 'I love you and I want to marry you.' He fell to his knees beside the bed and opened the box, placing it on the bed next to her. 'Will you marry me, Alice?'

She stared at the ring, then at him, stunned.

'You really mean that, Jeremy? This isn't some guilty reaction from the accident?'

Jeremy's expression turned from desperate to wry. He'd told her before that he kept forgetting she'd studied psychology. 'No, my darling Alice, it's nothing like that. I admit the accident opened my eyes. The thought of losing you that day nearly killed me. But I was already wildly in love with you before then.'

'You were?'

'I was just too damned scared to face it. But I'm much more scared of living my life without you. So will you marry me, my darling?'

Alice tried not to cry. She didn't think Jeremy would want her to cry. She stared down at the lovely ring he'd chosen. It was exactly what she would have chosen herself.

'Of course I'll marry you,' she choked out, picking up the ring and slipping it onto her finger. It fitted perfectly. 'Thank you, Jeremy. You've made me so happy. I... I...' Alice broke off as the dam of emotion she'd been trying to control suddenly burst, tears flooding her eyes.

'Oh, my darling!' Jeremy exclaimed as he leapt up and hugged her, and in doing so accidentally pressed the buzzer. They were both still hugging each other when the nurse hurried back in.

'Well, I see I'll have to go get the doctor,' she said happily. 'Then I'll see if I can find some champagne!'

EPILOGUE

St Paul's Cathedral. Twelve months later.

IT WAS SATURDAY AFTERNOON, just after four p.m. The weather was warm, but not hot. No rain in sight. All the wedding guests were seated. The bridegroom and his two best men were waiting somewhat impatiently at the head of the aisle for the bride to arrive.

'Alex said to tell you that he's brought the gun,' Sergio whispered to Jeremy.

Jeremy's head jerked back as he turned and stared at his two best men. 'What in God's name are you talking about?'

'You said if you ever fell in love,' Alex elaborated, 'that I was to shoot you.'

Jeremy had to laugh, which brought a mock glare from Sergio. 'Have some decorum. You're about to be married. Marriage is serious business and not to be joked over.'

'You can say that again,' Jeremy returned. 'I'm a bundle of nerves.'

'Not having any second thoughts?' Alex asked cheekily.

'Hell, no. Frankly, I've never looked forward to something so much in all my life. If I'd had my way I would have been married months ago, but Alice wouldn't have a bar of it. She said she wanted to be a June bride, with all the trimmings. She wouldn't even agree to move in with me, said I had to wait till she was Mrs Jeremy Barker-Whittle for that privilege.'

'She's one strong-minded woman,' Sergio said. 'But then that's exactly what you needed, Jeremy. You were way too used to getting your own way with women.'

'That's what Alice always says. And Madge.'

'Who the hell is Madge?'

'My PA.'

Alex nodded. 'Well, we all have to keep an eye on you,' he said. 'Women seem to fall in love with you even when you don't do a damned thing. I was down at the back of the church a little while ago and there was a row of attractive young ladies sitting there, chattering away, the subject of their conversation being what did the bride have that they didn't have. All exes of yours, I gathered.'

Jeremy smiled. 'I could have told them.'

'Then tell us,' Sergio suggested. 'We have to talk about something, given how late the bride is.'

Jeremy thought for a long moment, then sighed. 'It's actually quite difficult to put into words. Alice is an enigma. A contradiction in terms. Not contrary. But she has two sides to her personality, both of which I love. She's fire and ice. Light and dark. She's not perfect by any means, but then who is? But she's perfect to me. I love her stubbornness and her fierce independence. I love her compassion, and her passion. But most of all I love the way she fell in love with me, despite knowing what I was. She looked past the shallow life that I'd been living and saw the decent man that I could become.'

'The man you *have* become, my friend,' Sergio said admiringly. 'Alex and I are very proud of you.'

'Amen to that,' Alex agreed. 'Hey, I think your paragon has finally arrived.'

Whatever else they might have said was drowned out by the sounds of Wagner's 'Bridal Chorus' bursting forth from the pipes of the massive grand organ St Paul's Cathedral was famous for. All the guests—and there were over two hundred of them—rose as one to watch the procession down the aisle.

Once the music started up, all of Alice's nerves fled. The moment had come. Soon she would become Mrs Jeremy

Barker-Whittle. He would be her husband for life. Oh, how she loved that man, never more so than when she told him last month that something must have gone wrong with her mini pill—its failure possibly due to a gastric attack—and she'd fallen pregnant. He hadn't been annoyed or disappointed or put out in any way. He'd been thrilled, reassuring her that he hadn't wanted to wait long to have a baby anyway. They hadn't said anything to anyone yet. It was still early days, but the test had been positive. Alice herself was over the moon. She hadn't wanted to wait, either. And it wasn't as though she'd be fat for her wedding. If anything her pregnancy had made her strapless bridal gown fit her even better, her breasts already larger, filling out the boned bodice in a rather provocative fashion. In fact, she thought she looked quite sexy.

Harriet and Bella looked sexy too, in their own strapless blue gowns, made in the palest blue chiffon and draped to suit their shapely figures. Both of them had their hair up, their stylish buns decorated with the same tiny white flowers that filled the posies they held. Alice's hair was up too, enhanced with an exquisite diamond tiara that had once belonged to Jeremy's gran and which he'd inherited many years before but had forgotten about. Alice's bridal veil was a froth of tulle that reached down her hips. She had opted not to have a face veil. She didn't like that idea much.

Alice watched as her two matrons of honour preceded her elegantly down the aisle, smiling at the memory of the wonderful holidays the six friends had already spent together. She and Jeremy along with Sergio and Bella had joined Alex and Harriet in Australia last Christmas, along with their two little boys. Jeremy's namesake was by then nine months old, with Bella's son, Alberto, a few months younger. They'd also spent Easter together at Sergio's villa on Lake Como. What a lovely stay that was. They'd promised each other not to let a year go by that they wouldn't meet up somewhere, preferably somewhere warm and relaxing. The thought pleased Alice that next time she'd have her own baby with her to be admired and photographed.

'Time for us to go, Alice,' her mother said as she hooked her arm through Alice's. Her mother was giving her away, since she didn't have a father to do the honours. 'But before we do, let me say how very beautiful you look today.'

'You too,' Alice replied. Her mother was wearing a slimming ice-green coat dress with a matching hat. 'Jeremy said the other night that you were a dish, and that it wouldn't be long before some lucky man whisked you off to the altar.'

'Oh, that man!' she said, but she was blushing just the same.

Mother and daughter began the slow walk down the very long aisle, the glorious music echoing in the vaulted ceiling above them. Alice smiled at all her wonderful guests, who were many and varied. Along with relatives she never knew she had, there were all of Jeremy's rather large family, people from work, plus lots of women whom she had helped. Finally, she saw Fiona and Alistair, who both beamed at her, Fiona patting her small baby bump to indicate that she was expecting. Marigold and Jarod were expecting as well—next month, actually—which was the main reason Marigold had chosen not to be in the bridal party. She was huge! Dickie called out loudly to Auntie Allie whilst he jumped up and down on the seat, till Jarod swept him up into his big strong arms and told him to hush.

Alice hugged her own good news to herself, thinking how happy everyone would be when she finally told them. At last, Harriet and Bella reached the end of the aisle and turned left to clear the way for Alice. It was then that she spied Jeremy, looking his usual resplendent self in the black dinner suit he'd worn the night she'd first seen him. Alice had refused to let him buy a new suit, saying he couldn't look any better to her than he had in that suit.

He did look a little nervous, the poor darling, she thought as she drew closer.

There's nothing to be nervous about, she telegraphed to him with her mind as her smile widened and her eyes sparkled.

Jeremy should not have been surprised at how beautiful Alice looked. She was already beautiful. But seeing her dressed as a bride, in that divine ivory dress with its tight satin bodice and *Gone with the Wind* skirt just blew him away. She seemed to glide down the aisle, her smile the smile of sheer happiness. Emotion welled up threateningly within him, but he controlled it. No way would Alice want him weeping at their wedding. She needed her man to be her rock, not some wishy-washy waterworks.

So he pasted a smile on his face and prayed for composure. But his hand still trembled when he took her hand in his.

'You're nervous,' Alice whispered.

'Terrified,' Jeremy agreed quietly.

'Don't worry, my darling. I'll look after you.'

The archbishop cleared his throat and the organ music immediately died down.

'We are gathered here today,' he began in a voice to rival Jeremy's, 'to join this man and this woman in holy matrimony...'

Madge wept silently in her pew. Ken put his arm around her shoulder. 'Would you like to get married, love?' he asked her gently.

Madge stared up at him, then nodded, her eyes awash.

'Good,' he said. 'So would I.'

Alice's baby was a girl. In keeping with the tradition of floral names for girls they called her Jasmine Rose. She was the apple of her daddy's eye, exquisitely beautiful and totally charming.

Jeremy knew that from the time she turned twelve he would not have another moment's peace.

* * * * *

In case you missed them,
the other stories in Miranda Lee's
RICH, RUTHLESS AND RENOWNED
trilogy are available now!

THE ITALIAN'S RUTHLESS SEDUCTION
THE BILLIONAIRE'S RUTHLESS AFFAIR

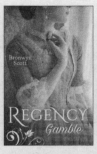

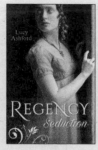

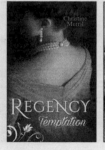
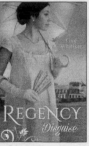